# ATTAINMENT

## BOOK 1 OF 3 OF THE
## ATTAINMENT SERIES

Chloe,
I hope you enjoy :)
J.H. Cardwell

J.H. CARDWELL

ISBN: 1489571345
ISBN-13: 9781489571342

# PROLOGUE

**Spring 2009**

He knew he was leaving, probably forever.

How did his life get so screwed up so fast?

Everything was spiraling out of control. His home life was over as he knew it. And, Reese...Reese had still not let him *touch* her.

When they kissed, his mind was exploding, and he couldn't take it anymore. He had so much pent up anger from just...life. Abstinence from her was making it all the more unbearable.

He thought he loved her, but what did it matter, he was leaving. He would be in Kansas tomorrow, and wouldn't ever be able to touch her again.

His older brother's friend had attained Rohypnol, and tonight he would use it. Who cares? Skip didn't even ask questions. He knew when he told him not to mention it to his brother Josh, he wouldn't. Josh on the other hand, would've killed him for even thinking it.

Reese wouldn't even know he'd done it.

She had a siren's song, and he couldn't leave without knowing what it felt like to be inside of her, totally consuming her. After all, she had been his and now a part of her would be forever.

She had said *no* too many times to count…determined to wait until she was 'married'. Damn. Why does she have to be so good?

So here he is, at the party…the loud, nerve racking, obnoxious party. All he can think about is how it will feel later. He just needs to slip it in her Coke. A little more than Skip had said, to make sure it takes effect. He said you couldn't taste or smell it. He better be right.

*I can't have her remembering anything tomorrow*, he thought, and with a little smirk of his face he turned up his lip.

She's supposed to stay tonight with her best friend, that bitch Elle. Why does she have to always be around…ugh. Somehow, I can convince Reese to leave when it starts to hit her some, and she can drive herself 'home'.

At least that's where she thinks she'll be going…

———

"Reese babe, you don't look like you feel so well."

He said, as he put his arms around her waist.

He can tell she is feeling very sleepy. She really just wants to go lie down.

"You're right, I feel really strange, kinda sick all of a sudden." Reese turned to Elle, her face scrunched up "I'm going to run home for a little while, but I'll most likely come over later and still hang out with you and the girls."

Reese leaned over, holding her arm across her abdomen.

"What's going on with you, did you eat something bad, or are you coming down with something? I'm sure your sweet *boyfriend* will take you home then?" said Elle.

He started fidgeting and looking around "Uh, I've promised my mom I would pick something up for her, I was planning to leave and come back, but I can find someone else to take her...you can't leave your own party Elle."

He knew they understood his house was in the opposite direction from Reese's.

"Guys, I'll be fine. I'll drive myself home, but Elle, I'll call you when I get home and let you know my..."

"How about you call me Reese when you get home? I'll have my cell phone on. Besides, I'd like to talk with you once more before I leave. You really aren't looking well. Elle, you won't be able to hear your phone anyway, with all of this noise."

Whew, he was starting to get nervous about how quickly the drugs would take full effect of her.

"Agreed, I guess," said Elle, "but please drive safely Reese. You really do look pale."

He left a couple of minutes after Reese.

She was sluggish, and it took her longer to get in her car and buckle up...much less start the engine, and navigate her way around the avenues.

Luckily for him Reese's windows were down, so he slowly pulled up beside of her, glad it was dark out so neighbors wouldn't see. He motioned for her to park her car in an abandoned drive he'd already scoped out.

He parked his a few blocks up, and ran back to her.

She was on the verge of knocking out.

His heart was pumping loud and fast.

"What's happening to me? I think I'm going to pass out," she said out loud.

He pushed her over a little, and slid in laying the cool, leather seat to her white Jeep, all the way back.

He made sure the top was up, and he rolled the windows up, further hiding themselves from the elderly neighbors. Hopefully, they were already asleep in their beds at 9:45 at night.

"Oh Reese, I've been begging for this for so long."

He started to gently rub her neck with his left hand, then quickly and roughly spread her legs, tightening his grip on her neck...his fear enhancing the aggressiveness in his movements. He started unzipping his khaki shorts, and rubbing himself with his right hand.

"Thank you, sweet girl, for wearing a dress for me tonight." He said with a deep growl.

"Reese how you turn heads... you need to be more careful not to drink an open drink at parties. You never know what might get slipped in there, with all of the guys watching your every move."

He continued to grope her hair, and slid his right hand down her perfect breasts, her nipples getting erect from the stimulation.

"See, I knew you wanted this, look how your body is responding." He had a dark expression on his face, sweat rolling off his tan features from his damp, golden, blonde hair.

He pushed his groin hard against her. "A little more time sweet Reese, and you're all mine...just a shame it won't happen again. I can already tell how good you're going to be."

Reese's eyes shot open like she had a surge of adrenaline, and she tried to push him off of her, but her hands and arms felt like they was asleep. It felt like she had been laying on them without moving, for hours. They were dead weight.

Her long, honey-colored hair trapped behind her on the head rest, keeping her from moving.

She grunted what she wanted to be a scream, but no sound came out. She prayed for it to stop.

"Oh be ready love, I am going to fill you completely. If only you would have said yes to me, you could be enjoying this too."

He was holding her wrists so tight above her head now with his left hand. Not that she had much of a fight in her, but enough to keep things from running smoothly.

He roughly kissed her mouth, almost gagging her with his tongue.

So many times in the past he'd tried to make love to her mouth with his...dipping his tongue and sucking her lips, but she always ended the kiss too early, and pushed him away.

Well not this time.

She tried to pull her knees together, so he shoved against her harder, nearly combusting from the anticipation.

He'd had sex one other time in his young life. A neighbor 'slut' as he called her, who willingly gave *it* to him. Although nowhere near as gratifying as this was going to be with a 'good' girl, a virgin no less, someone he really had feelings for.

His erection was hard. Pushing her panties aside, he slammed into her, as deep as he could go. He immediately felt warm and looked down seeing red.

No response... Reese was out cold.

"Oh shit Reese, you feel so good. No one can ever take this from you again, No one." Although in his mind he was cursing thinking but one day she would've given it to someone…

I woke up to a cold, lonely car.

Where was I? Why did I hurt all over, and why couldn't I really wake up?

I tried to gather myself and think clearly.

Looking at the clock, and finally getting it to focus… "2 am?" I shouted out loud (but it came out more of a whisper in the car).

My doors were locked, my windows up. How did they get that way? I was laid back with my seat reclined, my dress smoothed out down to my knees.

I slid up in my seat and screamed from the piercing pain I felt between my legs.

"Oh God what's happened to me? Please help me God? What do I do?"

# CHAPTER 1

**Summer 2010**

He snuck up behind her and wrapped himself around her wet clad, bathing suit body.

He pressed up against her shapely, tall figure. Pushing her long, honey colored hair aside he ran his fingers down her arms, kissing slowly on the soft neck area, directly behind her ear.

He gently tugged on her earlobe with his teeth. She let out a low, guttural whimper, letting him know this is what she wanted.

He was getting more and more arous....

"Tate, what the hell man?"

Everything came rushing back to him at once...as a football landed on his chest.

Hysterical laughter broke out all around him.

He scrambled to his feet slowly realizing what was happening, and that the group of guys, his 'friends', were all pointing at him.

He had gotten a damn hard-on, visibly showing through his dark blue UnderArmour swim trunks.

Uggh...*Why do I even have daytime dreams of her? I should give up already, he thought.*

It was all Tate could think about, her gorgeous body, long and lean. Her slender nose, almond shaped, green eyes, long golden hair, heart shaped, full lips, beautiful cheek bones that flushed ever so lightly, and her sweetness...oh her sweetness.

Tate turned to his friends, sweeping his muscular arms out in front of him, "shit man, y'all leave me alone. You just wish someone could tell if you were having a wet dream, by the look on your pants...assholes."

"Man what were you dreaming of, Romeo? Let me guess, Reese Stanford?" Finn yelled chuckling like a schoolgirl. "That's it. Look at his face."

All of the guys were laughing again. His buddy Jack bent over, unable to catch his breath from laughing, but Finn was drawing the most attention his way.

"Give it up already Tate, she doesn't like boys like that, hell she doesn't even like to kiss." Finn turned to Tate getting serious all of a sudden.

"Besides, with your following of chicks, she wouldn't want to, and you don't really need her to now, do you player?" Finn high fived all of his buddies, and sat down in the lounge chair beside of Tate.

"Have you heard that Carter Davis is back in town? He's back for the last month of our senior year man. I can't believe he would come back to school this late in the year... this close to graduation. This could change the game for you anyway with your dream girl...sorry man, but this sucks for you."

Finn turned to Tate and found a shocked look on his face. "I guess Reese didn't say anything about that to you did she?" He slapped Tate on the back.

Carter's dad, Tony, had moved to Kansas for a temporary military position. Since he and Carter's mom were having problems, they'd separated and Carter went to live with his dad.

"Man, why do you want to start up shit like that? I'm sure Reese just doesn't know it yet, you know. And besides, I don't think she still has feelings for him. As far as I know, they haven't talked in a long time."

Then Tate got close to Finn. "Uh, I didn't even realize Mr. Davis was back in town. I wonder if he and Lisa…I mean Mrs. Davis are getting back together? Oh never-mind. Anyway, I'm sure it won't matter to Reese about Carter now."

Finn leaned back and plopped his feet up on the table, looking like he owned the pool.

"Well, I find that hard to believe since they dated for six months before he left town with his Dad. Besides what is it they say about first loves? You should know Tate. I bet you never fully got over Lauren…even if she did turn out to be a cheater."

"Shut the hell up man. Okay so we dated awhile, and I thought I liked her, but she is not what I'm looking for man."

"Okay, okay, I get it. No more talk about your former *love*." Finn snickered out loud. "If you ask me, Carter's a tool. But Elle says the girls dig his straight lace appearance and Izod sweaters. He even wears loafers," he laughed. "Elle said he's a track star, and shooting for a full ride to UNC Chapel Hill."

"Damn, he's smart too."

After a few minutes of cooling off, Tate walked over to Reese, and grabbed her by the waist.

He could feel her flinch under his arms, and her skin tighten.

Tate wished she enjoyed his touch, but so far she seemed uncomfortable when they got too close.

"Hey babe, are we going to get pizza at Vino's tonight?"

Tate stepped back to give her space, and see her reaction. It also gave him a better chance to gaze into those gorgeous green eyes.

"Um Tate, I know we talked about it, but I um... have to change plans. I'm sorry. My parents' friends are back in town, and we have to go out to dinner as a family. Maybe tomorrow?" she said as she stepped forward to touch his arm.

Tate knew it was hard to disagree with her when *she* made the move to get close.

"Uh, Okay I guess...hey, can I talk to you for a second?"

He gently pulled her to the side where no one could hear their conversation.

Feeling unsettled Tate stared at Reese for a few moments. "Are you sure we, I mean you are okay Reese? When were you going to tell me our plans had changed?"

She seemed a little nervous to Tate, but still caring and sweet. "I really am sorry Tate. Of course we're okay. Why wouldn't we be?" She grabbed his chin and he thought maybe this was going to be their first real kiss, not just those sissy pecks she'd been giving. But she just gazed into his eyes, with a tender smile.

"Okay then." He said.

"I do have one more thing to ask you Reese..." He paused, "Will you please wear a cover up while you're walking to the canteen? You look so hot in this bathing suit, and I love seeing it; but so does every guy here. I've been watching them drool after you…"

"Are you kidding me Tate? They are not drooling over me! Besides, I just hopped up real quick to get a drink."

"Well just hop into your cover up real quick…It can't take too long." He said with an easy chuckle trying to keep the conversation light. "I just don't want guys thinking you're handing out an invitation, and I'm sure you don't want that eith….."

"Shut up, just shut up," she said as tears starting forming in her eyes. "Is that what you think I'm doing, inviting guys to take advantage of me?"

Elle overheard the last part and came running up to Tate.

"What the hell did you have to say that for Tate? Maybe you should just back off okay?"

"Wait a minute Elle. What I said wasn't really that wrong was it?" He looked confused.

"Well it is to Reese…never mind." Her concerned blue eyes were on Tate. "Just leave her alone right now."

"Wait Elle please tell her I'm sorry and that I didn't mean to upset her." He ran his hand through his hair seeming flustered… "Tell her I'll see her tomorrow."

Elle whipped her long strawberry blonde hair around and ran her pretty, petite, fair-skinned self after Reese. She was her best friend, everyone knew it. But since last summer they had been inseparable, and Tate barely had any time alone with Reese. He was hoping all of that would change over this summer. If only he could get her to open up to him.

I REALLY did like Tate. I had started to realize it more every day. I did think he came over a bit possessive…Elle assured me that was because he really cared for me.

I know he likes me a lot, but hopefully not too much. I didn't have too much to give, I thought with a sigh.

I loved how strong he was, and such a gentleman. He came from a good family that had a LOT of money, but he didn't seem spoiled. He was unusually respectful for this day in time; even if he was a gruff guy, ball player, and somewhat of a partier. He was gorgeous with that country-boy, tanned, muscular, hard-working build of a frame. At just over 6'2" he was a power house, but gentle. His eyes were dark hazel brown, with a deep inset, proving a strong forehead, and a movie star, square jaw. There was a lot of experience behind those eyes… but what kind of experience was always my question? Ugh, why did I have to be so hard on him? He calls me beautiful, and doesn't try to push himself on me. Maybe I should give him the benefit of the doubt, and spend a little more alone time with him to get to know him better. I had most definitely started falling for him. I was worried what that meant for me. If there was one thing questionable about Tate, at all, it was his jealousy. He was possessive, and sometimes overly so.

But I couldn't think about that right now.

I had to think of how I was going to see Carter again tonight, for the first time in nearly a year.

Why did he have to leave? And why did he lose touch so quickly? Surely there was someone else.

I got upset just thinking about it, and tears gathered at the corners of my eyes, threatening to spill over and ruin my makeup.

The time since he left had been an emotional roller coaster. First, the rape...the *rape* for God's sake...Why did this happen to me? Maybe I really was to blame. I had racked my brain trying to remember ever sending crossed signals to anyone. I had wanted to tell Carter about it SO bad, but I knew he would think of me as 'damaged goods'. I had told him NO to sex for so long, that he would wonder how I could give it up so easily to someone else. Oh he was smart, he would know I didn't offer it out, but I was no longer pure none the less.

It hadn't been my fault had it? I was drugged. At least that's what the blood report showed...enough drugs to put me asleep for a day. Luckily, I woke up and rummaged for my phone to call for help. Carter had sent me the sweetest text after he left me that night...(I cried just thinking of it)...*He texted he had wanted to hug and kiss me goodbye but was worried he would break down. He assured me he would see me soon...* but we both knew then, he was staying in Kansas until he left for college, after his senior year. I would only be able to call and text him. Maybe Face time, but that happened only a couple of times early after he left.

The detectives didn't pursue it too hard, because I begged my parents to let it rest. I was tested for STDs and pregnancy... both negative, thank God. I can't imagine if I had to have a baby now not even knowing who the father was. Moore High School kids would have never let me live it down if they knew.

They did take samples of skin under my nails...what little there was, and um, other samples of DNA. They said I really didn't put up a fight, because I was so out of it. There was no fingerprint match from the prints they had obtained from the door handle, and the steering wheel or DNA match in the system. However, they would flag it to alert them if anyone was ever arrested that matched the profiles.

For weeks, months even, I couldn't look guys in the face, not knowing if one of them was my attacker. No other girls had come forward claiming the same thing either... My parents had heard about a visiting school kid from a Northern Virginia high school, and thought he could have done it. He had a record of a previous date rape.

But his alibi panned out to be secure, and with the DNA not matching, that was a dead end.

My reputation would be ruined at Moore High if they found out about the rape. Small towns are notorious for spreading gossip like wildfire. Everyone would eventually blame me... They would just hear that I had had sex, and think of me as 'loose'. I shuttered thinking about it. There was no winning either way.

Maybe Tate was right, I really should be more modest...I never wanted to be 'asking' for trouble; although, I truly didn't dress like most of the other girls already. I wore modest shorts, and never showed my cleavage...too much trouble always worrying about falling out every time I bent down. My bathing suits are fairly modest bikinis, because I just can't imagine wearing a one-piece until I'm at least 40. I mean my mom still wears bikinis for goodness sake. No, I don't lead people on with what I wear, or how I act. I was sure of it. The Christian counselor my youth pastor had sent me to (and made me see) assured me it was not my fault, and that I wasn't being punished for having sex. I didn't choose it after all.

Still, I wasn't entirely convinced. I grew up loving God, but where was God when this had happened to me, and why should I be listening to a counselor who had never been through it?

I was scared to ever be alone now.

I never drove alone after dark either. Oh…how I wish I could go back in time. I would never have another open cup, always a bottle with a top…For that matter I would never put myself in that position again. I would stay away from social mixers, where guys and girls partied together.

To this day no one else knew, only my parents, the detective, my youth pastor, and the counselor (I still see once a month), and of course Elle knows…my best friend Elle. She had been my constant shadow since that night. What would I do without Elle?

# CHAPTER 2

"Hi Carter…I can't believe how much you've changed in one year." God that was stupid. I cringed at my own choice of words. I was meeting Carter again for the first time at dinner, at Coplan's Restaurant with our parents.

Carter put his arms around me, holding on a little longer than expected….sending my emotions all over the place.

"Reese, you look amazing…so mature…" Carter's gaze fell to my chest and caused me to immediately step back a little. I knew I had blossomed in that department, even more since he had seen me last.

"It's great to see you again…your voice even sounds a lot deeper, older" I said.

*I hope I'm not all the same in your memory bank,* thought Carter.

"I can't believe it has been a year already" I said.

I knew this meeting would be awkward…I just never expected it to be this much so.

He still never knew how drastically my life changed the night before he left…And as far as I was concerned, he never would.

Carter leaned over to my ear and whispered, "Hey Reese, want to go somewhere after dinner and talk?"

I froze for a second. Something familiar coming over me, and sending a chill down my back. What was it…was he still affecting me so? …I couldn't put my finger on it. But I knew I needed to tell him about Tate. Now was as good of a time as any.

"I know we probably need to talk about…things, but I can't. I mean not tonight. I um, have already promised a few of my friends…um girlfriends that they could hang out tonight in my Dad's cabin behind our house…" My dad had restored a vintage cabin making it a cool hangout…TV, fridge, covered porch, and best of all a huge hot tub underneath an arbor and usually a vast sky of stars… I was rambling to Carter, but I wasn't sure when or if to tell him that Tate had already asked me to hang out tonight, anyway.

"And Tate?" he said not looking away.

"No Carter. Tate won't be there either. But I think he is certainly something we need to catch up on…what made you ask?"

"I heard from some of my old friends that you two were dating. It's cool Reese. How could I not expect you to move on…you are a sexy, smart girl after all…I remember how you turn heads," he said in almost a whisper as he drew nearer to my face.

Something all too familiar flashed before my eyes "What did you say?"

"That I totally understand it…"

"No, the last part…"

He looked confused. "Okay, how you always were one to turn heads…"

I turned toward him looking at him for a long moment, wondering why that last sentence made my skin crawl.

Carter noticed she tensed up and had a questioning look...*what was that about* he thought. "Look, Reese, I wish I hadn't had to leave last year, and then, we wouldn't be sitting here talking about you dating someone else. It would be me...always me." He held her gaze and felt a deep, dark desire worm its way up his spine.

He looked away before he gave in to his emotions. What was wrong with him? He had come so far over the past year. He had kept his mind off Reese as much as possible keeping busy with track... running faster and harder each race, running from those memories...those awful memories. The guilt was eating him alive. But she seemed okay, from where he sat...and already moving on to another guy. Actually, the more he thought about it he started wondering if he had actually done her a favor...helping her loosen up a little. But he also started feeling jealous, and it was aimed at a guy he'd casually known for years, a guy named Tate Justice. Had he already convinced Reese to *be* with him?

"Carter, if that were true why did you drop off the face of the earth when you left? I had gotten your sweet text that last night I saw you." I had to keep talking so I wouldn't get drawn in to that dark time "Then each one after that seemed forced, fake even. What was going on with you?"

He squirmed in his seat… "You know why I left. I'm sure your parents told you. I just couldn't talk about it…not even with you. My parents were separating and my mom was blaming my…"

"What do you kids want to order?" asked my mom, interrupting us. "Sweetheart, do you want the fillet cooked medium, we can split an entree?"

My mom, Liz was elegant and slender, light brown hair with golden highlights, green eyes, like me, and looked 10 years younger than she should. She was always worried for me and always talking to me in her honey voice (even more so since last summer). She was a devout wife and heavily involved in our church. Always looking up to my Dad, and trying to be the best for our family. They had a great marriage. Sure they fought occasionally, but never long in front of me, and they always seemed to patch it up quickly. My mom was cool too; she liked hanging out with her friends and having cookouts. She drank a glass of wine every evening…She said it was her 'liquid Xanax'.

"Yes, that would be great mom, with a side of asparagus. Can I get my own salad though…with balsamic vinaigrette dressing?"

"Sure sweetie."

I turned my attention back to Carter, who had just given his order to the waitress. He was staring at me. "Can I call you later, and we can take this up where we left off…since I can't see you later tonight?"

"How about Saturday morning? I'll be trying to sleep in, but maybe we can grab coffee at the shop around the corner from my house. Say 10:00?"

Now that we had a meeting time and place, I wasn't sure what I was doing. Tate would be hurt and probably furious. After all, I hadn't even told him about Carter being back in town.

"Saturday," he said with a wink. Two days away he thought. Can I wait that long to be close to her again?

# CHAPTER 3

That night was great just to hang out with the girls. Elle had come over as well as Maura and Chloe. They all lived near my neighborhood, and were members of the club pool. But mostly they loved the cabin and the hot tub. We watched 'What Not to Wear' eating our popcorn and drinking Diet Dr. Pepper. Then we plunged in the hot tub.

"Y'all are a bunch of lushes you know that?" I said casually, cracking a smile and leaning in to Elle.

"We're dying to hear about your dinner date with Carter tonight… you two-timer you," said Maura half -jokingly, half serious. They were all upset with Carter for giving me the cold shoulder last year. And they all seemed to love Tate (some-times, a little too much).

"Well for your information, it was not a date. We went with our parents, and we were barely able to talk and catch up," I said, with a grimace on my face. I realized I was just now able to let out my breath, after worrying about seeing Carter all day.

"Did he talk about his parents being back together any," asked Chloe? "I heard Mrs. Davis had shown up to work with bruises last year, a few weeks before Carter and his dad split town. When she was asked about them she just broke down crying."

I couldn't imagine the woman sitting a little ways across from me earlier tonight, being that weak, and having problems that severe last year. Mr. Davis, I thought...was he the reason for the bruises? He did sit tightly beside of her and she kept a stern look on her face the entire evening. In fact her mouth stayed in a flat line, she never seemed to smile. I thought they were back here to reconcile. I made a mental note to ask my mom about her good friend Lisa Davis, and what her story was for real. Mom always said Lisa and Tony were just too indifferent and couldn't seem to make their marriage work. I also wondered if it would come up with Carter when we talked again. Maybe that was the real reason for his drawing away from me.

"That is the absolute first I have heard of that Chloe. I sure hope you have your information wrong." I said as I turned to Chloe. "Who told you that?"

"Let's just say it is a VERY reliable source...and I would believe anything this person tells me about it." Chloe snapped her fingers in a 'z' pattern like she meant business.

"Besides, why are you so worried about Carter anyhow? Leave him be for someone else to have a chance with. Believe me you've got the hottest ticket with Tate. Don't screw that one up. Someone might be ready to pounce on him if you turn your back, even if it's only briefly to spend time with Carter. I hear Lauren is asking around about Tate again. You know they have a history. One you have yet to have with him." Chloe seemed proud of herself for throwing out her opinion on the matter. She had her long, brown, thick hair up on top of her head in a loose bun. She was splashing around in the hot tub in her too tiny bikini. She really was a lot of fun…just always sure to speak her mind.

As it goes, we were all very close friends, and basically grew up together. Chloe was the wilder one of us, always with lots of stories to tell. I felt like we spent the majority of our time trying to tame her. Maura was extra book smart, and very matter of fact, but also very crafty. She could come up with a solution to anything. Especially when the four of us needed to get out of a 'situation', like getting home too late from shopping and eating afterwards or something of the like. But usually, Chloe was the reason for our 'situation' anyway. Elle was my best friend, and had been since the 5$^{th}$ grade when we joined forces on a project, and came out with a victory…and a blue ribbon. We had spent hours at each other's houses preparing our board and power-points. She was always loyal and would take up for any worthy cause…bullied kids…the poor, 'whatever for the weaker' she always said. We leaned on each other for practically everything.

"Listen, y'all know how much I like Tate. He is the only guy besides…"

"We know. He is the only guy besides Carter, that you have ever given the time of day," said Chloe. "But let me just say, there is something wrong with that too. You could have any guy at our school Reese…but if you don't stop acting so damn snotty and goodie two shoes you won't have anyone." Chloe stared at me dead on.

"Look, I'm not saying to get down and dirty with Tate, but girl you have to loosen up a little. Do a little exploring with each other if you know what I mean." Chloe was rolling her head, getting a little too relaxed in the hot tub.

Elle turned and looked at me. "Okay, maybe we should call it a night. I'm exhausted, and I'm sure Reese has had enough advice for one night."

I secretly planned to thank her later for that rescue. I don't want to talk about intimacy of any kind…much less the exploring Chloe was meaning. They don't know what happened to me last summer, and I'm not about to exploit my fears, not even to my close friends. They can focus on their own love lives or lack there-of.

"Hey, before we leave," Chloe announced. "Finn asked me to mention a party at his house tomorrow night. He wants us all there. There will be a keg of beer and lots of good music." Chloe said as she was twirling around in her fluffy bath robe (we each had one at my house just for frequent dips in the hot tub). We also each had beach towels with our names on them. That was my mom's idea, but we loved them.

Elle eyed me and gave Chloe a scary, mean look. "I thought he told you to tell *me* about the party. You act like he was asking you to come."

"Don't get your panties in a wad Elle. We ran into each other leaving school yesterday, and he just threw it out there. I know you have your sights on Finn, girl. I think he digs you too. But remember what I said to Reese. If you mess around too long without making your marks on your man, they will move on." Maura chuckled at what Chloe was saying. They all knew Chloe never held back.

"I say if they aren't happy with what we give them, then the hell with them." I exclaimed as I sauntered to the sunroom door. "But I will give you this Chloe, I guess I need to do a better job of letting Tate know I care about him…life just gets difficult when history comes back to bite you in the ass."

Chloe couldn't help it "Ooh, maybe that will happen literally, you know, bite you in the ass," and we all burst out laughing.

"By the way, I don't plan on going to that party. I say we come back here and have a repeat of tonight." I was hoping they would agree with me.

Chloe pouted, and even Maura and Elle gave a whiney face.

"I'm sorry, you know I don't do parties with booze…too much of a chance for trouble…not to mention those dang phones with cameras and the pile of mess they can get you in. Maura, you remember just a few months back don't you?" I asked.

Maura covered her face with her arm. "How can I forget? I may never live down someone taking a picture of me after I had had a couple of wine coolers, leaning over Brian Rierson like we were about to do something. God knows that wouldn't have happened with HIM in a million years." They all laughed, but knew it was serious.

Elle announced she was coming back there after Reese's date with Tate. Then they all agreed, although a bit reluctantly, to hang out in the cabin. Elle gave me a wink, saying more without words than either Maura or Chloe could imagine.

~~~

"Make sure you invite Reese and her friends to your party Finn," Tate hollered. "I want to bring her over after our date."

"Don't worry man I've already mentioned it to Chloe, so she would tell the girls. But I hate to break it to you, she's probably already got plans with Carter." Finn gave a cheesy grin and punched Tate in the arm. Tate punched him back.

Finn fit his name to a 'T'. He was the good-looking surfer type. Sort of a 70's looking hippy for the 21st century. He was tall, muscular, but not bulky muscular like Tate. And he had hair nearly shoulder length that he always kept in a ponytail. He also had a couple of tattoos already. His parents gave him free reign and he perfectly abused it. He was always having parties. As wild as he was, he was twice as loyal. He always bailed out his fiends…especially if he was the one that got them into trouble in the first place. He knew every hard rock band from the 90s and loved to go to the concerts, always dragging his buddies along. Pretty much he was the life of the party. Luckily with all that partying, he kept good grades and was great at baseball just like his best friend Tate. They too grew up together, and had been stuck like glue for years. Finn was planning on a Wake Forest scholarship for baseball, just like Tate.

"I mean you heard they went out to eat last night, right?" Finn asked as he marched over to grab a basketball and shoot some hoops. Tate had the coolest house in the neighborhood. His parents were both lawyers and they could afford the best of everything; including a true basketball court beside their four car garage.

"Man you're yanking my chain. Reese would have told me about it…hell, she would have asked me first, surely." Tate said as he did a layup and swooshed the ball. He just knew Finn had to be wrong…wasn't he? All of a sudden, he felt Reese slipping through his fingers. He couldn't wait for dinner tonight to probe her about such crazy accusations.

"I'm not worried about tonight anyhow; I know Reese wouldn't see Carter after a date with me. She's not like that."

"Don't hold your breath man. They have a lot of history... Elle says they were in love."

Tate's eyes grew angry and dark.

"How in love could they have been if she started dating me?"

Finn gave a little laugh "he blew her off, that's how. But now he's back and I'm sure he will play it up like he didn't like the distance. Look man, I don't like him, I mean there is just something about him...but I will say, be careful Tate, you can't mess with history."

Tate turned to Finn "unless it's bad history, then you run from it."

"I'll be glad to help you kick his ass if you want." Finn started jumping around punching in the air like he was boxing. "You know he would never mess with her again, if we just taught him a lesson."

"I'll keep that in the back of my mind Finn. But I know if that happened and Reese found out, I would probably lose her anyway."

No, he wasn't going to plan to beat him up...for now, but he would get to the bottom of it. As Finn said, there was just something about Carter that he didn't like.

# CHAPTER 4

As usual, Vino's smelled like pizza and steak and cheese subs. It was the hang out of many a nights after games. Basketball season was long over. Now baseball was in full swing, and nearing the end. Their team won the Thursday rivalry against Belton High. Tate was the number one hitter and second baseman. There were scouts now at every game, with Tate and Finn being a shoe-in for a scholarship. Tate was hoping and praying it was for Wake Forest so he could go there with me.

I tapped his arm (he had insisted on sitting on the same side of the booth as me like we were in the 50's). "What are you thinking about Tate?" he gazed up as I spoke, with what appeared to be contentment and what…love?

"Just about us Reese and how glad I am you came with me tonight." His eyes were so endearing. "Also, how happy I'll be when you tell me you'll let me take you to Finn's party after this." Tate had a goofy grin plastered on his face…He didn't seem to acknowledge the group of giddy girls that had just passed our booth, hoping to grab his attention with their short skirts.

I turned to face him. "Tate, you know I don't do parties. Why do you keep asking me? Why don't you ask one of your other girls…you know the ones who worship you?" I glanced over my shoulder, "they obviously love to party."

Tate winced like he had been punched in the stomach. "Is that really what you want Reese? You want to push me in the arms of another girl? Or is it I'm the one not good enough for you?"

Ouch, that stung. What is wrong with me? I reached over and grabbed his hand rubbing my thumb over his knuckles. "I'm sorry Tate I shouldn't have said that…Of course I don't want you to go with someone else…I just don't do those types of parties anymore. I know I used to…"

"I know Reese, what happened to you? What changed you so much since last year? I guess I don't understand."

"Look, I don't want you to worry about me. I actually had already planned on having my girlfriends over again tonight. We didn't get to do the pedicure thing last night after we got out of the hot tub, so we want to make up for it tonight."

Tate squeezed my hand and slid a little closer to me. He raised his eyebrows "hot tub…now you're talking…what time should I be over?"

I slid my hand over Tate's and threw my head back. I felt the same electricity I used to feel when Carter held my hand, only I can honestly say even more so with Tate…

He put his arm around my shoulders and whispered in my ear "I guess I should be glad you aren't coming to the party then. I won't have to worry about fighting dumb dudes. I mean that dress is amazing Reese. I'm sure I wouldn't be the only one to think so." He was leaning his head up to mine.

"Oh please, Tate. You have all the guys scared of you. Nobody would even glance my way" I said, confident that I was right.

"Um, I know of one who would."

"Really, who?"

"Carter, he's back home right? Why, I'm not sure. Is there something you want to tell me Reese?"

My heart started to race…it really was innocent wasn't it? But if it had been so innocent, why didn't I tell Tate about it already? My emotions were bordering a breakdown. I could feel it.

"So you already know?"

"About your dinner date?"

"It wasn't a date Tate, I swear…."

Tate spoke quickly cutting me off. "I know it wasn't a date Reese. You were there with parents. But, why didn't you tell me? I am an adult now, I can take it… I didn't say it wouldn't hurt, but I want to know what you're up to. I really hate having to hear it from someone else." He looked around at me when I dropped my chin towards the table.

I flinched with his words. I hated to hear he had been hurt by me.

I looked up at him and rubbed his cheek softly with my hand. "Do you think we could go outside and stand for a little while? I really don't want to have this conversation in here. Okay?" I wasn't sure what I wanted, but I did feel like I wanted to be honest with Tate. I did love having him near me. I didn't want him to feel like I didn't.

"Sure. Let me pay and we'll go outside," Tate said.

We walked out quickly…Tate's hand resting on my lower back. The night was seasonably warm and the stars had just begun to cover the sky. Tate ran ahead and turned the radio on to a Kenney Chesney song, and rolled his windows down. We leaned up against Tate's new white, Ford F-150. I felt so good being with him, relaxed and safe.

He reached over and pulled me in front of him, his arms low around my waist. "Is this okay Reese? I want to hold you and look at you while we talk."

Was it okay? Of course it was okay. My God how I loved the feel of his biceps rubbing up against my arms…Wait, did I really just think that? I have to admit I felt unusually safe in his arms.

"Of course Tate…" I instinctively batted my eyelashes." I like this," I said as I lowered my head to his firm chest. We swayed to the music.

"Well, I hope I don't regret asking about this, but what are your feelings toward Carter?"

"Wait, before you speak," Tate's words were slow and measured. He reached for my chin and held it softly between his fingers. "I have to tell you I don't know if my heart could stand for you to still be emotionally involved with him Reese. I don't think I have to tell you that I'm falling hard for you. You are everything I ever wanted. You are sweet, loving, beautiful, kind. You come from a great family of wonderful values, and I know you have big goals to achieve," he swung his arm slowly in the air to insinuate endless possibilities. I tried to speak but he put his finger to my lips "Reese you are all I need. Please think about what he did when he just left you hanging. He broke your heart. And I would kill him if he did it again…hell, I should kill him for doing it the first time. I have had this sort of bad boy meets good girl image since we met, but seriously…I can't think about you hurting."

Oh Tate, if you only knew, I thought. There was a long silence.

"Now can I talk?" I lightly chuckled as he took down his finger. "I thank you for saying all of that about me. I think that *you* are amazing. How did I get so lucky to have you want to protect me? I…" I reached up and put my hands on his chest again. "I really do think you are pretty awesome." I couldn't stand it anymore…his words…his actions…I reached up and kissed him. I left my lips slightly parted and then the kiss grew firmer, more intense. He lightly caressed my tongue with his tongue and put his strong hands on both sides of my neck drawing me nearer.

Our bodies seemed to melt to one. No one else seemed to matter. It was like I couldn't get enough of him. I felt his breath catch, and his hands seemed to tremble on my face. Oh Tate, do I really do this to you? You could have anyone else you want. We continued for what felt like minutes, until he inched his body against mine, and I felt like I couldn't take it…I forcefully drew back, my eyes wildly searching his.

"Oh my God Reese, are you okay? That was…that was amazing. I…I can't tell you how much I've wanted you to do that. Why did you stop? Oh God, do you regret it?"

After a few seconds of catching my breath I looked up at Tate "Of course not silly, I…I really enjoyed it…actually…" He started to move in closer again for another kiss but I put my hands out to distance us. He said "okay, that will have to be enough for me tonight I guess. I'm sorry Reese…I didn't mean to push you for more. That was just…Wow…I guess I feel better now about our talk of Carter, after *that*."

"Speaking of Carter, Tate, I promised to meet him for coffee in the morning, and I just wanted you to know." I looked down at my feet, then reached up and grabbed two handfuls of Tate's shirt.

"Seriously…Ahh, why do you have to see him at all?" Tate looked down at me with a pained look on his face.

"Well, I guess I wanted to have a little closure, you know. Find out what was going through his head over the last year. There is something different, I can't explain it." I looked up at Tate with expectant eyes.

"Okay, but will you call me afterwards, you know so I know everything is ok…with us?"

"Don't' worry Tate. It's never been better," I said as I leaned up on my tip toes and kissed him one last time.

# CHAPTER 5

"Details girls..." praised Chloe. "I want details. Come on"...she was pointing to Elle and me "who had the best date? I guess I mean who has the juiciest dish?"

"Well, mine was great, but nothing fancy or romantic really...we just ate at Bill's Bar-B-Q and talked a while." Elle shrugged her shoulders. "But hey, we didn't even plan on doing anything until a few hours ago, so I'm just glad we went." She smiled, still remembering them holding hands when he stood to help her out of the booth.

"Oh good grief...Reese please tell me you have better gossip to give than that?" Chloe waved her arm towards Elle, gesturing that her news was just plain pitiful.

"Well...I guess you could say that..." I shyly dropped my chin as I spoke in almost a whisper. Then I let a huge grin play across my lips. "We had our first real...I mean *real* kiss...you know tongue and all." They gasped all around. "I mean, I will have to say...that it was truly sweet and sensual." I brought my fingers to my lips with lingering thoughts of the last hour.

"Ooh...now that is what I'm talking about." Chloe high fived all the girls.

"Okay, enough…" I said still giggling and swaying towards the hot tub. Let's take our usual dip and then do our nails. My mom has snacks in the kitchen for us too. And, she let me set her iPod out on the deck. What shall it be…you know she has a rockin' playlist…Van Morrison or 38 Special?"

"Thank God for your mom and her taste Reese…I would have never experienced the 80's or 90's if it wasn't for her," said Maura laughing out loud.

I was enjoying my 'Girls Night In' all the while thinking about that kiss and if I was honest, I was also thinking about seeing Carter tomorrow. Had I been wrong to tell Tate? Really, am I wrong to be meeting with Carter? Uuhh…I let out a long breath.

"Hey, so I wonder what they're all doing at the party at Finn's?" said Elle. I know she had really wanted to go. Sometimes I wonder if I shouldn't loosen up a little. I had already decided maybe the next party I could go for a little while. I had also decided I would open up a little more to Tate. Maybe kiss him like we did earlier tonight again tomorrow. *That* was so nice…. more than nice.

"I'm sure they are emptying the kegs as we speak. I would love to be a fly on the wall around where they all get their beer. That's where they do all of their gossiping. More gossip than us girls," said Chloe.

Afterwards we painted our nails in the cabin and started watching 'Pretty Woman', a movie out of my parents' movie collection. Chloe had brought blueberry lemonade wine coolers that she had gotten from her cousin, who was already in town on summer break from college. Maura wasn't drinking. She would be the DD and drive Elle and Chloe back home in a little while.

"Hey girls, I'm getting tired. You know it's never as fun when I have to sit here and watch y'all have fun drinking." Maura gave a half chuckle, half aggravated sigh.

"I get it Maura, it's after dark and I'm pretty tired. Besides, this is the third time we've seen this movie. I love Julia Roberts and Richard Gere, but luckily I know the happy ending..." Elle said gathering her purse. "We've already seen the part where he catches her flossing her teeth and thinks she's doing drugs." We all laughed.

"Yeah, I bet there was some of that at Finn's tonight too. Although he would kick someone's ass if he caught them doing it. He and Tate hate that stuff." Thankfully, none of us ever tried drugs either. So many in our class had...what will they do when they go to college and can do it freely? They'll get into so much trouble. Lots of people don't ever finish college if they get hooked on it. "That girl Skylar Lincoln had to be sent to rehab last year for cocaine. She won't even get to graduate with us," I said. "Let's make a pact to *never* do drugs. Ok?" Everyone agreed. I was confident that none of us would screw up our lives like that. Well, I was hopeful at least.

"You guys go ahead. I'm going to finish watching this, then I'll lock up and head in, I've still got to get my mom's iPod in too." I was still laid back in my bath robe on the mini sofa in the cabin. "But text me when you get home so I know you made it ok? I have my cell phone right here." I raised my cell phone up and shook it in the air, then sat it back on the sofa.

After everyone was gone, I totally relaxed, finishing off my drink, feeling a little light-headed, but definitely relaxed. I was replaying my time with Tate, when I heard a soft knock at the door. Must be my mom I thought. Oh I hope she doesn't get too mad about these wine coolers. They've said I could drink at home but not anywhere else...since I'm about to graduate and head off to college. I guess they figure I'll probably have some there. My mom says at least she won't have to worry about me hiding it from her if I'm so adamant about doing it sometimes. I guess I would be the same way when I have kids. My dad says if you are old enough to fight in wars, you should be responsible enough to make choices about drinking.

Without checking (what kind of idiot doesn't check), I opened the door half jumping out of my skin when I realized who I was looking at. Carter was standing at the door, with his hands in his jean pockets, looking cute and shy as ever. "Crap Carter... you nearly gave me a heart attack...how...I mean what are you doing here?"

He just gazed at me. His look went right through me. Then he gave me a once over, eyeing my fluffy white robe that came mid-thigh, then finally his eyes came back to my face. "I didn't mean to scare you Reese, I've just been thinking about you since last night, and how I need to talk with you."

I took a few steps back. "I was expecting my mom that's all..."

"Do you mind if I come in for a few minutes? I promise not to stay long...are you watching a movie?" He walked in the door with his hands in his pockets, looking like he was nervous.

I sat down on the small sofa all the way to one end. Not realizing it, I had sat down on my phone. I also didn't realize that I had 'butt dialed' the last person I had spoken with...

Tate. Carter sat on the other end opposite me, but with the sofa being so short it didn't put him longer than arms-length apart really.

"It was so good to see you yesterday Reese," he reached over and brushed his hand against my knee, appearing accidental. He noticed I cautiously moved my legs together. "I wanted to finish talking about my parents, although it's still kind of tough to talk about." He had a strange look about him when he mentioned his parents. I'm sure it would be so hard to have your parents separate. "They are back together…at least you could call it that. We're all living together now. Josh (Carter's older brother in college at NC State) will even be coming home this summer. Anyhow, last summer my mom had an affair. Everyone said my dad deserved it, you know being cheated on, because he was not a good husband. But, I don't give a shit, you shouldn't cheat." He seemed to almost spit that last part out.

Carter's face was getting red just talking about it and he was getting a little loud. He stood up and started pacing…I just sat still listening with guarded apprehension.

"So it seems my dad got rough with my mom when he found out, and made a few small bruises on her…I don't know, maybe when he was trying to shake some sense in to her…It seems he was shocked and disgraced by the cheating, but even more embarrassed and angry by who it was," he said.

"*I* still don't know who it was and my dad refuses to tell me. He says he thinks it was all of my mom's doing…that she came on to the guy, but I say the guy was probably a stalker and made her. Anyhow, she made my dad leave and had promised it was over…their marriage done."

He was looking at me now with genuine...what was it fear, sadness, I couldn't quite read him.

"I was furious at both of them, I don't know, at the world too, but I couldn't live with her...she had caused the most wrong of the two...she abused his trust...she gave up on all of us when she cheated. So, I had to leave."

He started slow, calculated steps toward me.

"I'm so sorry Reese...if I could do it over again," he grimaced "all things over again, I would."

He sat back down beside of me again, this time a little closer. My emotions were falling all over the place. I wasn't sure if it was the drink making me feel fuzzy, or the information he had just handed me... he had willingly left and deserted me when really he should have needed me the most.

"I didn't know Carter. You know my mom and your mom Lisa are good friends. I guess she didn't want me to think badly of her, you know?" I dropped my chin and reactively said, "I had something terrible, AWFUL happen to me too, the night you left. I mean, my life changed forever. I will never be the same. I wanted to talk with you about it so badly, but you shut me out..." Should I tell him I wondered, I mean he was my boyfriend then? What will he think of me? It doesn't matter, he wouldn't have been there for me even if I had told him then "Never mind Carter...you left that's all, that alone nearly devastated me."

⌒

Carter was shaking with anticipation. Was she going to tell him what she thought really happened to her that night?

He wanted to make sure she couldn't see through him, and gauge the reaction on his face for what it really was...guilt. "God, what I would give for another chance with you Reese. Is it too late?" he reached up and touched her face with his hand...

# CHAPTER 6

ate was seething. It took him all of 30 seconds to realize what was happening on the other end of his cell phone. He was at Finn's and had to dart outside to hear it play out.

"Oh my God, that bastard" said Tate.

He ran up to a buddy out on Finn's deck (where the keg was) and borrowed his cell phone, all the while listening to the garbage on the other end. His blood was boiling. First of all, she had lied to him...she *was* seeing Carter tonight. She had brushed him off after their date to spend time with HIM! He dialed Reese's home number.

"Hello Mrs. Stanford...Can I speak with Reese please?" He exhaled a long, slow breath still trying to hear the conversation between Carter and Reese.

"Oh hi Tate, it's nice of you to call, but Reese is still in the cabin. Her friends left just a little while ago, she should be in shortly. You can try her cell, or I can leave a note for her to call when she comes in. We were just heading up to bed."

*So that is where he is with her.* "No, that won't be necessary Mrs. Stanford. I'll just call or text her. Thanks again."

His hands were trembling...still listening to Carter shamelessly explain things to Reese and ask for another chance...

he had to get there NOW! He ran for Finn and asked who the DD was for the evening. It was Luke Freeman. Good, Luke wouldn't ask any questions.

They raced to Reese's…it was about a ten minute, horrid drive…

⟡

"Carter, I can't do this. I'm sorry to hear about your parents and God knows I'm sorry to hear about you having regrets about us…I always wondered what was going through your mind. But I'm with Tate now. I can't just tell him goodbye just because you came back into town."

He looked like he had been slapped. He straightened suddenly. Then like another thought hit him he slowly moved in to kiss me. I didn't realize what was happening, until it was done. His lips touched mine, sending familiar waves through me. I knew I was ultra-relaxed from the drinks, but I didn't realize how slow I would be to react. He started to open my mouth with his tongue and I reared back. He almost fell on me he was so intent on finishing his kiss.

"Carter no…why did you do that? I can't… I won't kiss you." I was shaking my head, desperately trying to control the situation.

"Come on Reese, at least once for old times' sake…I have always loved the coral red bikini on you, it just does something to me."

I whipped my head around, "how do you know what color my bathing suit is? Then slowly it registered with me "you were here before, watching us… Or what Carter, how did you know?" Oh my God, are you kidding me? What did he hear while we were all outside? I mean where was he hiding?

He backed up a little, realizing he had just told on himself. "I, uh, I came to see you earlier but your friends were here with you...so I...uh didn't want to interrupt...I just needed time alone to talk with you, so I waited until they were gone."

"Oh my God Carter, you are freaking me out a little bit here." I pulled my robe a little tighter. "I think you should leave. We can talk about this...um when I have on clothes," I was pissed "and when I haven't had...Um I mean when I'm not so tired." I didn't want him to know I had been drinking. I wasn't sure why, I just didn't want him to know.

Just then the door flung open and Tate jumped on top of Carter crashing him to the floor. I had no idea what had just happened.

I screamed and jumped back. "Tate, no stop, what are you doing? Please stop!" My scream was piercing. They were wrestling, and Tate was pummeling Carter who I don't think had caught up with who was fighting him. I didn't know what to do. I was scared to jump in, but I didn't want either one getting hurt. The next thing I knew my dad was jumping in between the two of them breaking it up. They were swearing at each other, and both were bleeding...Tate from his mouth and Carter from his left eye. I couldn't think, I couldn't even breathe.

"Reese Stanford...I don't know what is going on up here, but I expect you to head to the house right now! I am very disappointed in all of you," he said, no he shouted. I rarely see my Dad so angry.

"And you guys...what are you thinking, fighting like this? Do I need to call someone to come get you?" My dad, Cole Stanford, was a muscular, fit and trim man. He kept himself young at heart by working out year round, and keeping a tan in the summer months. He also kept fit playing adult sports on the church baseball and basketball teams. He was over 6 ft. tall and was an architect, mainly commercial, but had designed his share of homes in the past. He was a man's man in every sense and he knew how to instill fear.

Carter took off in his car and Tate had to wait on his ride to come back. All the while, my dad drilled him on how he expected more from him. "I better not ever hear you have touched my daughter using that aggression son, I just might kill you if you do. Do you understand? If you only knew how fragile Reese is..." He stopped real quick realizing he shouldn't say anymore. "I will make sure Carter hears this out too...don't ever treat my daughter with disrespect... I have a gun and I am not afraid to use it Tate."

I had walked slowly back to the house and heard every word my dad had said.

Just then Luke was back...but I was sure Tate had lost any buzz he might have started out with. I know he couldn't stand for my father to be angry with him. And worse, I'm sure he couldn't stand the thoughts of the lingering sounds of the cell phone action, playing over again and again in his mind. I knew this was not the end of it. Knowing Tate, he would take care of Carter one way or another. If he had his way, I'm sure he would see to it that Carter never touched me again.

Riinnggg…Riinnngg…

"Hello?" Liz Stanford was barely awake, confused and fumbling for the phone at 3 am.

"Liz, oh God, Liz are you there? I'm out of my mind and I need to talk with you… Oh it's awful… Carter,…he's not good…oh God, he's not good at all. He was in a car accident. Oh Liz, they don't know what's going to happen to him…I… I'm scared to death.

"Ok…Ok…I'm here Lisa. What…where is Tony? Is he there with you? Liz turned on the lamp trying to get her bearings. She looked over at her own half asleep husband.

"Yes, he's here…he's on the phone with Josh. I…it's just… I don't know if he's going to make it Liz.

"Okay honey….listen, I'll be there shortly…Baptist right? Okay, I'm on my way…hold tight. I love you Lisa…hang in there…I'll be praying for Carter.

Liz hung up and shot out of bed in a flurry… "Cole…Cole, wake up…it's Carter…he's been in a car accident. Do you hear me?" He turned over half dazed shaking his head yes. "I'll wake up Reese and see if she wants to go with me. I'll call in a little while."

"Oh no, Ok sweetheart. Oh that's awful. Do you want me to go with you?" He said with his brow furrowed. He was wondering if it had anything to do with what had happened there earlier.

"No honey, you go back to bed. I'll call you in a little while okay?"

"Sure… I um…I'll pray for Carter and for Lisa and Tony. Please call when you know something."

Liz rushed in to Reese's room "honey, wake up…It's Carter…he's been in a terrible car accident. Wake up honey."

I rolled over dazed with my arm over my head… "Mom, what's wrong? What time is it?"

"It's Carter honey, he's hurt…hurt real bad…he…he was in a car accident…"

I shot out of bed "What! When? Oh my gosh Mom, is he okay?"

"Yes honey, I'm sure he's in surgery by now. Lisa says it is really bad. I'm heading to the hospital to be with her. Do you want to come?"

"Sure mom, I…Oh my God, I want to know what happened..and…and how bad it is? Give me five minutes and I'll be down."

My heart sank for Carter. I threw open my closet, and found jeans and a t-shirt and slid on Rainbow flip flops. I brushed my teeth in a fury, and threw my hair in a pony-tail. "What have you done Carter? Why were you driving so late?" *calm down Reese, I'm sure he'll be okay.*

We sped to Wake Forest Baptist Medical Center where Carter was in surgery. Lisa had said he broke his left collar bone, left radius bone, and had crushed his left foot. Evidently he had wrapped his car around a tree, and smashed the whole left side of the car in. The airbag in his Toyota Tacoma deployed, but he still had a severe concussion, from hitting the window. They weren't sure of the over-all internal damage, but these injuries they were sure of. They were enough to warrant his condition being critical.

"Mom hurry! What if he doesn't make it? Oh Mom…" I had calmed down enough now for the realization to sink in…*what if he dies, what if he is hurt for a long, long time. What am I supposed to feel or say to him?*

The twenty minute car ride was mostly filled with silence. Just as we arrived, my mom reached over and laid her hand on my knee. "Sweetheart, I know you are hurting for Carter, but be careful, don't let your emotions get in the way of how your heart reacts."

What? What in the heck was that supposed to mean...but I just nodded, making a mental note to ask my mom later what she meant by that.

# CHAPTER 7

The hours crept by at Baptist hospital, waiting for news on Carter. Finally, an anesthesiologist and surgeon came into the waiting room, relaying to us that Carter was in ICU now, resting in a deep sleep. The surgeries had gone according to plan, and we would need to wait. Mrs. Davis was allowed to go back to see him as was Mr. Davis. His brother Josh, who had finally arrived, had to sit in the waiting room with us.

I didn't truly know how to feel. Carter had just come back in to my life after over a year. He had very little explanation for why he had distanced himself from me on every level. He was acting strange, and he was acting kind of freaky…but still, I did have feelings for him…feelings that went back to last summer. As I sat across from Mr. and Mrs. Davis in the morning hours, I wondered how they were really doing? Who did she have an affair with, and what was the extent of it? I realized it was none of my business, but for some reason I was drawn to their problems. Maybe I felt it would give me a greater understanding of why Carter withdrew this past year.

Either way, I was here…here at the hospital waiting…waiting for Carter. Tate had texted me a couple of times. He was worried about me after the incident in the cabin, but I could also sense a little animosity. Around 8 am I had called Elle to fill her in. She had learned from Finn, that Tate heard my whole conversation with Carter. She said he was hurt and angry that I had kissed him...*Me kiss him*...and that he had other concerns about things that Carter and I were talking about. Those damn cell phones. I hadn't 'butt dialed' anyone in a long time. Of course it would happen last night. I try to do the right thing, and BAM, the unthinkable happens.

I thought through everything that I had said, and vice versa to Carter. The thing that worried me the most was what I almost said to him. I couldn't recall just how far I had gotten about my night before Carter had left last year. But, I was hoping Tate didn't pick up on any of that.

Then there was the kiss...that damned kiss. I didn't do it... Carter did. But would Tate see it that way? And, at this point, did I want him too? I mean he tried to kill (well at least beat up) Carter. Ugh, what was it with the guys in my life.

Sunday was a blur. Despite the encouraging words from the doctors, Carter was touch and go. Apparently he had gone home after leaving my house Saturday and ran in to a heated argument occurring between his parents at home. He fled their house, and was going 85mph when he took a curve, 'Dead Man's Curve' no less, and wrapped his car around a tree. Thank God there were no other cars out at that time of night. For Carter's sake, thank God he wasn't drinking.

Either way, he would forever be changed, the extent not nearly known. For now he was in a drug induced coma, because they were still unsure of his head injuries. They had encouraged me to sit and talk with him, but I didn't know what to say. Things had gotten out of hand with us just last night.

In fact there hadn't been an 'us' in over a year. Still, I sat in his room, and talked with him about college and sports and life... urging him to keep fighting.

After 20 hours of coma, Carter finally starting stirring, He was slowly moving his head from side to side and gently tapping first his pointer finger of his right hand, then his right toe. Mrs. Davis ran to his side, encouraging him to wake up.

His first words were 'I'm sorry'...at least that's what it sounded like he said. 'I'm sorry' for what Carter? Wrecking your car? Driving too fast? Coming on to me? Leaving your parents? What? Then he said "Reese". I was sure that is what he said...no one else could hear it, but I knew...What Carter, what are you sorry to me for? But, just as quickly, he drifted back to a deep sleep.

Another day passed before he finally was opening his eyes enough to keep awake. He still had a serious head concussion, so they were keeping him heavily sedated, until the swelling went down on his brain. His bones were healing from the surgeries. However, his nerves in his left foot and around his fractured left tibia were his biggest concerns. The doctors said he would have problems with the feelings in that leg, and that he might have what is called 'drop foot' which would cause him difficulty walking and especially running...Running! What about his scholarship to UNC?

Tate texted and called, and I completely avoided him. I wasn't sure why, except I knew he would not be happy with me being at the hospital every day for Carter, and we would argue about that. For some reason, I felt obligated to be there. I would have done the same for Tate, but I knew telling him that wouldn't make him feel any better about the situation.

On the fourth day, I had gone in to Carter's room, visiting with his mom and there was a knock on the door. Mrs. Davis softly said "come in..." When the door creaked open, Tate was walking in. I just knew Mrs. Davis would charge toward him, maybe even blame him for her son's thoughtless behavior that evening of the accident. After all, Tate had tried to beat him up. But she didn't, she gingerly walked to Tate who had his eyes set on me. She ushered him out the door quietly, and he was eagerly summoning me to come to him. I wasn't sure what to do, so after a minute I went to help rescue Tate. The door had been left slightly cracked, but when I opened it further, I found them a little ways down the hall. Mrs. Davis had her hand on his shoulder, talking softly in his ear. He was shaking his head from side to side and seeming very nervous, impatient even. I couldn't quite grasp what was going on. I didn't even realize Tate knew Lisa. Then I saw her lean up and give him a kiss on the cheek, and put her hand on his chest, sliding it down the front of his shirt.

What the hell...I don't get it? Tate leaned back on the wall and let his head fall back, while she walked toward the nurse's station.

Tate looked up and saw me, I'm sure I had a confused look on my face...what had just happened? He slowly walked toward me... "Reese, let's take a walk *now*..."

"No, Tate, could you tell me what is going on? How do you know Lisa?"

"Reese, please, let's go somewhere more private."

Tate grabbed my arm coercing me to follow him, I protested the entire way. When we finally ended up in an empty waiting room, he released my arm. He stood near the door, to block any way for me to exit. I paced back and forth not knowing what to say next.

Tate broke the silence.

"Why are you avoiding me? You can't just ignore me forever Reese." He ran his hand through his hair, with a look of exasperation. "I'm going crazy here…what do you want me to do, I'll do it…I just want you to hear me out…Please Reese, can we talk?" He was rambling and I knew he was upset. I had completely ignored him. I guess I deserved a little anger from him.

I was beyond furious, and more confused than ever. I wasn't sure what to do. I wanted to be there for Carter, because he was seriously hurt, but did I want to *be* there for him physically, emotionally?…I hadn't convinced myself that he was sincere after leaving me last year, withdrawing from me in my darkest hour. I mean as far as Tate goes, I was really falling for him, but could I love a guy who was so possessive and who wanted to basically own me. He didn't seem to be the kind of guy who would want 'damaged goods' for long once he discovered what I was really about.

I guess it was time I told him I knew why he had come over to get Carter. "Tate… I know you heard Carter talking to me over my cell phone Saturday night. I can't imagine how you were feeling, but I didn't invite him over. He was…uh… it seemed he was aware when I was alone. I'm not really sure how we ended up just the two of us, but there we were. And, he wanted to talk about old times and…" I turned to Tate, to plead in a way, "Tate, I didn't kiss him back. I was a little buzzed okay." There now you know, I thought.

Tate had stopped pacing the room and stared cold in my direction.

"I know what you're thinking, but I never planned to drink around anyone but friends and then he showed up…You know me Tate…I don't do that."

"Wait Reese, I do know you, and I do know what I heard on my phone…He wants you back and he kissed you…Didn't I have a right to kick his ass? I mean he had his chance to…Ugh, I can't take this anymore."

Tate nearly leapt across the room smashing into me.

"He had his chance Reese, now it's mine." He whispered breathlessly.

With that he kissed me, hard, pushing my back against the wall. All of the frustration from that night and the last few days fueling his fire. I protested at first, then gave in to the sweet, desire of his kiss. His soft lips were pressing firmly against mine, then he deepened the kiss by separating my lips with his tongue, and slowly caressing my mouth and tongue. The kiss seemed to last for…forever. This beautiful man *really* wanted me. His hands started moving up my sides. Oh my God the passion in this kiss. I was just as eagerly moving my lips and tongue against his. I had completely submitted myself to this moment with him. Our breathing deep, and hard, and fast. Then the door swung open, and the moment was stopped abruptly…like a record.

Lisa Davis stood staring…speechless. She looked from Tate to me, then swiftly turned and stormed out the door.

"Oh God Reese, I'm sorry about that kiss, I'm not sure what came over me…No, I'm not actually, I'm not sorry at all…I want to kiss you…please say you're okay with it…don't go back to Carter. He doesn't deserve you."

Once I got my bearings I was ready to retaliate. The kiss was absolutely divine, full of passions past the horizon,

Oh I wanted to be okay with him and all that has happened between his jealousy over Carter, and this 'whatever' it is with him knowing Lisa. But, could I be?

"Tate, what is it with Lisa...huh? Why...I mean I'll ask it again...How do you know her?" I straightened out my t-shirt down my front trying to compose myself.

Tate looked like a lost boy. He wasn't sure what to say. He started pacing the floor. I couldn't imagine what I was about to hear. I was a little nervous. Did I want to hear what he had to say? I had a really bad feeling about it.

"It's a long story Reese...one I promise you don't want to hear..."

"The hell I don't, you want me to talk with you, you have to do the same Tate."

He let out a long sigh and ran his hands through his hair. "Well...you know how Lisa and Tony split up last year...."

The door flung open again "Oh there you are Reese, thank God. I was getting worried about you. Everyone is looking for you, Carter is awake honey...He's asking for you. Didn't Lisa tell you?"

Momentary relief washed over my face. "Really Mom? That is great. I'll be right there. Go ahead and tell him I'm coming."

Tate reached out and grabbed my arm. "Wait, I want to ask you about something too Reese... something about what you were saying to Carter Saturday night." His face was getting red just thinking about all he heard, and what he imagined happened...with Carter kissing me.

"I've got to go Tate, let me go...please."

"Wait..." he stared into my eyes gently grabbing both of my hands and leaning his head to my forehead. "Please don't leave like this Reese. I've never felt about anyone the way I feel about you. But, I'm worried…about you. Something happened last summer…something you were about to let Carter in on, but I know you haven't shared it with me, because you told Carter it was awful, and horrible. Those were your words Reese."

I found it hard to breathe. I looked deep in to his eyes. I could feel it….love I thought…love for Tate, the way he clung to me for his next move, his next breath. But as quick as the wall started to fall, it shot right back up.

"Tate, you don't know what you're talking about…I…I've got to go. Please," I motioned to the outside "go, do your homework, or spend time with your friends…I don't know just…" and I turned and walked out the door.

"I am where I want to be Reese, with you…" he yelled in the air.

As I was walking down the hall, I didn't know what the future held for me and Tate, but I knew I had to keep my secret. I had to.

# CHAPTER 8

Carter was awake.

I quietly walked into his room, and found everyone standing around Carter's bed. My mom ushered me over to his side so I could talk with him. He looked so weak and his frame actually looked small, lying in the bed with tubes and lines coming out from all angles of his body. Tears started gathering in my eyes as Carter's feeble hand reached over and grabbed mine.

"Reese."

Carter's voice was barely a hoarse whisper...

"Hi Carter...we're so glad you're awake." I looked around the room meeting warm eyes to everyone in the room...everyone except Lisa, she was looking at the floor.

"Hey...could I have a moment alone with Reese?" Carter was barely able to speak.

"I think you need your rest honey," said Lisa.

"Mom please." Carter took what looked to be a very difficult swallow.

Lisa and Tony turned to leave, as did everyone else in the room. I wasn't sure I wanted to be alone with him yet...I couldn't wrap my head around my feelings, but I knew I wouldn't know what to say.

Carter patted the bed weakly with his hand, motioning for me to sit by him.

"I have to tell you something Reese," he said.

I swallowed hard.

"Carter we don't have to talk now. Like your Mom said, you need your rest."

"Reese...oh God Reese so much has happened... I guess you heard, I may have ruined my chance to run for Carolina... and with that my scholarship may be in jeopardy. I...I...am... Arrgh... Shit, it hit hurts so bad." Carter covered his eyes with his arms, his shoulders shaking.

"Running was my outlet. My dad will talk with the scholarship committee. He thinks they'll let me come with the understanding, that if I can't run after six months of therapy, then I will have to forgo my scholarship."

I just sat there stunned, listening to him. Of course, my mom had told me, and she thought this would happen, but to hear him say it, and to see the torture on his face trying to accept it, was just plain awful. I wanted to cry for him.

"Carter, what were you doing driving that fast, and where were you going?"

He looked all around trying to avoid my face. "I was angry Reese. Angry at Tate, not just for hitting me," then he looked me square in the face, "but for loving you like I should have done."

Did he just say that to me NOW after all the time when we were together and all that time he didn't even call, now that I have moved on...he loves me? "Carter...I...I don't know what to say." I looked down at the floor. Oh my God what does he mean, the way he should have…and…and Tate loves me… how does he know?

"How do you know Tate loves me?" Why was that my first question?…I guess subconsciously that is the one I wanted to know the most. Does Carter wonder why that was my first question too?

He paused, and looked disappointed. "I heard my mom telling my dad."

"I don't understand. Why would your mom be talking to your dad about Tate? Were they worried for you…I mean with me?"

"They weren't talking about it Reese, they were yelling about it…She was trying to convince my dad that Tate wasn't in love with *her*, that he was in love with you." His eyes were staring a hole in me.

"What? What do you mean not in love with…"

Oh…I felt like I had the wind knocked out of me. Surely I wasn't hearing what I thought I was hearing. I mean Tate…Tate was Lisa's affair? What? When?

I stood quickly, pacing the floor. "Carter, I think you must have it wrong. I mean, Tate and your mom would never happen."

"I'm sorry Reese, but it did…although my mom swears they didn't have sex…but I know Tate had to have. He's a player Reese, and he always will be. If they hadn't had sex, my dad wouldn't have been so upset, you know? Reese, I don't know when it started or how long it lasted, but my dad has all kinds of confirmation that they were together."

"Stop, I don't want to hear anymore…I… you have to be wrong…"

Lisa and Tony walked in the door. I couldn't speak. I certainly couldn't look at them. So I casually said, "now hurry up and get well Carter, so you can go home," like a babbling idiot. Then I turned and ran out the door.

My thoughts all ran together...Tate what have you done?... Could it be true? How have you kept this a secret from me?

Are you still seeing her?

Oh my God. I burst out crying...my heart broken.

# CHAPTER 9

y mom was starting to worry about me even more so than normal. I wouldn't eat, I couldn't sleep, and I wasn't talking to anyone except Elle. I'm not sure why, but I was still attempting to do my senior project. With just two weeks left of school, I had to turn it in. But I couldn't focus. I guess there was no more questioning whether I loved Tate or not, the answer was evident in how much I hurt.

Carter was receiving 'get well' messages from me, through my mom. I couldn't stand the thought of going to the hospital…sitting in the room where my world had crashed. In the end, I'm not sure if Carter was glad he told me after all. Because, it did drive me away from Tate; but, I also withdrew from everyone, including him.

I had managed to avoid Tate at school all week, with Elle's help. I had to break down and give her what little I knew of Tate and Lisa. She was furious. She knew though, I didn't want to give Tate the satisfaction of knowing what was wrong. So, she didn't really kick his ass, and drag him around school like she threatened…

My mom knew to filter my calls…I took more showers, ran more errands, and was 'asleep' more than I should have been…At least that's what information my mom was giving those who called.

Images of Tate and Lisa kept popping in my head. I wasn't sure why Tate would see someone that was married, much less nearly 20 years older than him. I mean there is no doubt that Lisa is gorgeous and in better shape than most college girls. But, she was MARRIED! It just didn't seem like Tate at all, not the Tate that I had known for so long now.

He sent me text after text asking me to call him, or talk to him…each of which I didn't respond.

The last text from Tate I couldn't help but read…it was in all caps and read:

> I DON'T UNDERSTAND WHAT I DID REESE BUT PLEASE GIVE ME A CHANCE TO FIX IT.
>
> I CAN'T LIVE WITHOUT YOU.
>
> YOU WON'T LOOK AT ME,
>
> YOU WON'T TALK TO ME,
>
> YOU WON'T EVEN TEXT ME.
>
> PLEASE REESE.
>
> GIVE ME ANOTHER CHANCE.
>
> I'M DYING….

I gave Elle permission, to pull Tate aside at school, and tell him that I couldn't see him now. She would tell him I had too much going on with school, testing, and packing…I had gotten my parents to agree to let me to go to Elle's beach house with her for two weeks, after graduation. I needed to get away…After that, it would only be a few weeks before I would be gearing up to go to Wake Forest. The class schedule that starts in late summer would be grueling and keep my mind off all back at home. Hopefully, by the time Tate started at Wake, he would have moved on to someone else. My heart hurt just thinking about it. I wanted to cry…again…but I truly didn't think I had any tears left.

Then there was Carter, I felt bad for not going to see him. He was in rehab several hours a day, so at least he was busy… but I don't know, I figured if he had lived carelessly without me for the past year, I could do the same now.

It was safe to say my world was upside down on its axis, and I was miserable.

Tate was throwing things around in the gym after Elle had her little talk with him. It took everything in her power not to slap him and tell him how much of a disgrace he was.

He was begging her to elaborate. "Elle, you have to tell me…I can't keep living like this…the not knowing is killing me. It has to be Carter…" He looked so crazy, so desperate. "She is, isn't she, she is seeing Carter…he's made her not see me anymore?"

I'm not sure when it clicked, but Elle saw this as her chance to get Tate out of the picture all together…which meant he would quit upsetting Reese, by trying to reach out to her.

"Tate, you're right…it is Carter. But, please, don't tell Reese I told you. She made me swear that I wouldn't." It actually was Carter. At least he was the one that had dropped the bomb that blew up their relationship so it wasn't totally a lie.

Tate was seeing red...He had at one time secretly felt sorry for Carter, because of his dad's brutality. But now, now he hated him with all things evil. His heart had been crushed and squeezed until it was completely broken in two.

How could he go on?

"Elle, why?" he said in almost a cry. "What kind of hold does he have over her? I don't understand it." Then as if he couldn't stand it anymore he turned and said, "I'll see you around."

In some ways, she wanted to run to him, and tell him she wasn't really serious, and that Reese wasn't with Carter. That Reese was actually dying inside, just like him. But her feet felt frozen to the ground...unable to deal the truth.

# CHAPTER 10

raduation finally came. I was able to act happy for my family's sake. It was a freeing feeling to be done with high school. Although I officially became an adult last October, when I turned 18, I now really felt ready to be a *grown up*.

It was great being around my friends for pictures, and actually laughing...That had been a foreign concept for over two weeks now. Tate had stopped texting. On one hand, I was relieved that I wasn't being tortured by his ever-presence pain...on the other hand, it hurt knowing he was moving on so quickly.

Carter was able to graduate on time, although he didn't get to walk in cap and gown. For that matter, he didn't get to attend graduation at all. But the most important thing was he got his diploma. He was going to Carolina...I was assuming I wouldn't see him again; at least not for a long, long time.

Of course I did see Tate at first, at graduation. But, we managed not to make eye contact. He spent most of his time with his group of guys doing what guys do...the whooping and cracking...We did lock eyes one time. I was mesmerized by the pain behind his eyes. I couldn't stand to look long, I turned my head. If I wasn't mistaken there were tears in his eyes.

I saw his parents, and they insisted on giving me a hug and getting a picture. Then they wanted one of me alone. I felt so foolish standing there cheesing for their camera. They asked for me to hang around until they could find Tate, and get a picture with him, but I acted like someone was waiting on me. I waved them bye as I took off. I have always liked his parents. I wondered what they thought had happened to us.

Life had already handed me more sorrow and twists and turns than I could have ever imagined. My counselor says 'that which does not kill you makes you stronger" and "God only allows you to have as much pain as you can handle." I guess that's true because I'm still standing…just standing no longer with a heart. Mine had been ripped out twice now. All through high school my friends told me I was so lucky, so beautiful, and that I could have anyone I wanted for a boyfriend. I guess that theory backfired. Maybe they're laughing right now, who knows. Because the truth is, if I hadn't been given the chance to fall in love, I would have never had the chance to discover what it feels like to be crushed by love. It is utterly exhausting to bend over and pick up the pieces of my broken heart. I let out a deep breath.

I guess it's true. Life can only begin when you start living. It was time for me to do that now, and get out of this funk that I had quarantined myself to.

After all, we were going to the beach today! I was actually getting a little pumped about spending all of my time relaxing on the beach. Emerald Isle Beach was a beautiful, quiet para-dise. Elle's family had a house in Sailman's Point. I called it the Charleston rainbow, subdivision of North Carolina. All of the houses were fairly new, and each painted a different color. And, just like my neighborhood on the avenues in my small town of Penderton, Sailman's had a golf cart to each home. Only at the beach, each home had a private pool and a hot tub. Elle's home was luckily beach front. I was going to be in pure bliss. It would be a shame to bring my pities with me when we got there.

Just as I was leaving with my parents, walking in a sea of dark blue gowns and groups of families; someone reached out and grabbed my hand, yanking me behind the wall near the parking lot. Before I could scream, I caught a look at my perpetrator.

Tate.

"No, I can't do this...Tate no..." I was shaking my head so hard I thought I might fall over.

"Reese." My name came out of his mouth like a hiss, like he had literally been holding his breath the last couple of weeks, until now.

"Please, I need to talk to you," he said.

"My parents will come looking for me soon. You are already on my dad's shit list remember?"

"I remember...maybe I'm trying to get him to shoot me like he threatened. I would probably be better off."

"Tate, I was sure you had gotten over me. Thankfully you had stopped texting and stopped calling. You didn't even try to find me anymore in school."

"Gotten over you..." tears stung at Tate's eyes. He found it hard to breathe with Reese being this close. He wanted to hold her, hug her, kiss her... "Reese, I can barely breathe without..."

"Reese where were you...Tate what are you doing!" My mom all but screamed at Tate. "We didn't know what had happened to you." My mom realized Tate had been crying. She reached out and grabbed his hand. I quickly turned the other direction and starting walking off. "Tate, this isn't healthy for either of you. I don't understand it, but Reese must have a good reason for breaking things off with you. You need to respect that."

"Mrs. Stanford, you know the reason…she is back with Carter. I'm not supposed to know that, but I…I was told anyhow." The desperate look in Tate's face made her want to help him out. She knew Reese wasn't seeing Carter. But she bet there was a reason he was told that. She would have to talk with Reese about it later today.

"I'm not sure what is going on with Reese? Maybe her time away will be good for her."

"Time away, what do you mean? Where is she going?"

"Oh, me and my big mouth…Um, she is going with Elle and the girls to the beach for a while."

"A while, how long is that?"

"Tate, probing me about Reese is not the right answer. This is between the two of you."

"I would agree, if she would talk with me. She won't even respond to my texts."

"I'll talk with her Tate, but I certainly don't expect it will do any good. I am her mother after all. The most luck you will have will be getting through to her with her friends." She winked at him and patted his hand, then turned to find Reese.

After my mom grilled me about Tate and Carter for nearly an hour, we were on our way to the beach. I decided to drive, because we loved having the Jeep Wrangler at the beach, with the top down. It was my favorite way to travel in the summer... unless it rained of course. I had to ask for new homework assignments more times than I would have liked; because, mine got soaked from an afternoon thunderstorm, that had popped up out of nowhere. North Carolina was notorious for those.

Thunderstorms reminded me much of my life...everything going just peachy with sunny skies and extra hot temperatures, then bam, out of nowhere the storm of the century tears it all apart. Leaving limbs and rubble in the path to clean up. My counselor says that it is our growth process...we don't know the best way to work through problems, if we haven't experienced them. And that one day, we can use what we have learned to help someone else in the same situation, dig their way out quicker. I just wish that job would be dealt to someone else. Let me be the one to help someone learn how to have the easy, less turbulent life. Now that would be better.

Maura had helped me to start praying again. She didn't understand why I had backed away from that in the first place, but she was sympathetic. She had learned to turn to God with her problems after the picture incident, and the way kids at our high school had treated her. She says there is comfort in knowing God is always there, ready to listen and provide peace. I guess at my age, I just pray God will help me figure out how to have fun again.

# CHAPTER 11

Truly the ride to the beach can be some of the best parts. We were all so happy to be done with high school, and on to higher learning...yeah right. We were so glad to be on our own! We gossiped and laughed and talked about all of our plans for the beach and the nights. We even got pulled over on the way to the beach for speeding. We were so distracted, talking about all of the people and parties that would happen at college. Luckily the policeman was enjoying having pulled over four 'now college girls'...and the fact that Chloe was doing all she could to throw her cleavage in his face. He let us off with a warning. Thank goodness, because my dad would make me pay for my own insurance if I got a ticket. We turned the radio up and all but stood and danced (well the top was down, so I think Elle and Chloe actually did...long after we left the cop).

The beach was A-Maz-Ing! I truly needed this peace. Well, I guess you could call it that. Elle, Maura, and Chloe had planned out the entire two weeks...partying, partying and more partying. Our parents didn't have to come along this trip - one, because they knew us, and trusted that we would look out for each other, and ALWAYS have a DD if we drove away from the beach. And two, they knew we were all 18 (I would be 19 this year), and in a couple of months would be on our own at college anyway. This was sort of our trial to see if we could make it. Also, they knew Emerald Isle was as quiet and low key as you could get…not Myrtle Beach on any level. They even had several extra sets of eyes from other home owners at the beach, neighbor's they had known for years.

I guess I should have expected that the girls would have our time all panned out. After all, this was their senior 'weeks' too, and they weren't wallowing in a desolate tunnel of despair, like me. In fact, Elle was seeing Finn a lot more regular now. She was rather smitten by him and his charm. He was a cool, good guy who had a similar following as that of Tate with girls, but he seemed to be good with one right now…Elle.

I had secretly talked with Elle about staying alone for a few days after the two weeks were through. I guess I can look forward to that. Her parents aren't planning a trip to the house until late July. By then I will be at Wake Forest studying my heart out. I'm not sure how I would get home, but I will work that out when the time comes.

I had a long, private talk with my mom. She told me what Tate had said to her, and that someone had told him that I was with Carter. I didn't know if I should let on that I didn't know what she was talking about or not. I had a feeling I knew where the gossip came from…but I would handle that later.

For our first night, we had plans to go down to Beaufort by the dockside. Beaufort is one of my favorite places. My parents have a fishing bungalow across from the Cape, and when I was growing up we would travel the 30 minutes to Beaufort or Morehead City for nicer restaurants and shopping or other entertainment. We would always go for a walk, gazing at the hundreds of enormous sailboats docked near the boardwalk. For many, this was a midway stop for them as they leisurely sailed from the North end of the Atlantic to the South end. As a kid, I always wondered what type of people could afford to do that, but I always wanted to experience it. Heaven on the seas, my Dad called it. On special occasions, they line all of the sail boats with mini white lights. The illumination across the water is striking. Many of my childhood pictures are at the docks at Beaufort. Carson's and The DockSide are two of my favorite restaurants there, and every night in the summer they have live music on the boardwalk. Emerald Isle was a 30 minute drive in the opposite direction, the difference was we were ocean front in this house, and in my parents' house, we were sound front and had to drive further than Beaufort for the beach with waves and 'ocean'. Or, we could have taken our boat or a ferry to the Cape.

After a couple of hours of primping and dancing around the house to music, we were finally ready to leave. Tonight it was Maura's turn to drive. We drew names for each night of the week so there would be no arguments. The local landscaper had a son in his early 20's. He had agreed to be our purchaser of alcohol while we were at the beach. We would give him money and extra tip for making sure we were well covered. The restaurants were a different story. Since we were under age, we couldn't buy it ourselves. Chloe was hoping we would always have a tall, dark, handsome, stranger cover our bill, but you couldn't always guarantee it. As for me, I choose only to have something when it is just the girls. I am still spooked about drinking in public. The problem is, if I have a drink before we head out, I get a little to laid back to make that kind of critical decision if someone offers me a drink. So…I have to have back up plans. One, whichever of us is the DD, that person has to make me not drink out in public. And two, if I am too weak to adhere to rule one, I have to see the bartender fix it and keep my eyes on it at all times, with the help of my friends. Of course Elle is the only one who knows all of the reasons behind these crazy rules, but Maura and Chloe believe they are just helping me stick to my old, stupid rules for life.

Elle was giddy over all of the texts she was getting from Finn. If I had to say it, maybe even a little premature, I would say she was in love. Of course, she won't let it on to Finn. She is 'just having fun' as she puts it. I know they haven't had sex yet, and I hope they keep it that way; although, if they keep this up, they can easily be boyfriend/girlfriend at Wake.

Maura hasn't had a steady boyfriend since her incident with the picture a while back, and Chloe, well, Chloe has had a couple of fast relationships, but nothing serious. I will be surprised honestly if she ever gets married and settles down. But, who knows.

Truth be told, we are a force to be reckoned with anywhere. We all take pride in our looks, and we LOVE to have a good time. We are usually the loudest ones in a restaurant, and by the time the others leave, they are either cussing us out of pure jealousy, or laughing along with us.

# CHAPTER 12

We had a delicious meal at Carson's, and then we walked over to the boardwalk to hear some live reggae-type music. We each had on cute, little dresses and either stilettos or wedges. I of course, chose stilettos and as I walk on to the boardwalk, I am reminded why stilettos are such a bad idea here (another reminder would be to look around at all of the flip flops and deck shoes). Shit. My heel got stuck in between two planks of wood on the boardwalk, which is built much like a pier, or a very long deck. How embarrassing. The other girls keep walking, until they realize what has happened. I'm laughing, but secretly trying not to cry. These are my favorite tan heels that go with absolutely everything. I quickly realize I can't take it out without ripping off the lower half of the heel, the black step part if you will. So Chloe, already a little tipsy from drinking on the way in and two at the house, yanks may arm and my foot comes out of my shoe.

As we're laughing hysterically, I reach down to grab my footless shoe, when I feel a warm hand lay on my arm. At first I'm terrified, my laughter ceases immediately, while the other girls are almost doubled over. I look over to see who in the world is attached to that arm, when a gorgeous dark haired, blue-eyed, beach god is staring back at me. He has on a white t-shirt, blue jeans and flip flops. Deliciously divine. You can see the rippled smooth muscles beneath his thin, white shirt.

"Excuse me miss," he says with a sexy grin "but I believe you lost this." He reaches over and grabs my shoe and without any dismemberment of the shoes parts, he hands me my tan heel.

"Oh I…thank you," is all I can muster. Then I quickly say "but it wasn't necessary, I could have gotten it."

"Reese," Chloe says to me, leaning over her mouth turned to the side as if to hide her whisper; although, he could plainly hear her. "What are you doing? Don't you dare walk away from him! Introduce yourself for goodness sake. I mean, isn't that what you came here for, a little R & R from your real life. If you don't, I will!" And at that I knew she would.

"Chloe, go ahead, you have my blessing. I have my shoe. I want to listen to music." So I keep walking to head toward the sound of music. Secretly praying my friends would pick up the stride right along with me, and not stay to talk to him.

Chloe hesitated, and seemed to be fighting the biggest inner struggle…good vs bad…but in the end she huffed a big breath and ran to catch up to us.

"Thanks Chloe…I always knew you had it in you to pull through at the last second…and you proved me right."

"Bitch," she chuckled. "You owe me. He was the hottest little thing I've seen in years."

The music was wonderful and relaxing. We swayed to the beat…even dancing a little as the music got at its loudest.

Chloe is right, this is exactly what I needed…sans any Beaufort, mysterious man.

By the time it was nearing midnight, I was exhausted. Between graduation, seeing Tate, driving, and Beaufort, I was ready to call it a night.

I was about to see if the other girls were ready when my phone buzzed.

> Reese, I hope you are having a good time at the beach with your friends.
>
> Please be safe.
>
> I miss you. You can't imagine how much… Tate

Oh Tate, I do miss you. How does he do that? He is taking the high road, but I am on to him. Why did you have to be such a jerk…so unlike what I thought you were? I mean how do you willingly participate in an affair? And what were you thinking? I saw you for the family man…wife, kids and all of that. Did you ever stop to think Lisa already has a family? I can imagine she has no interest in having more kids. But, I'm sure you thought of that. You were probably just using her for the time being, like so many other guys do…like the jerk who date raped me! Shit, why am I getting so worked up over this? We broke up, I have moved on. But still…I miss Tate. And if I'm truthful I miss Carter a little too. Ugh.

"Hey guys, I'm beat. Are y'all ready to head back?" I asked, realizing I was having an argument in my own head. I was officially over-tired.

"You know I am," said Elle. "I wanted to talk with Finn real quick when we get back to the house."

"It's after midnight Elle, can't you wait until tomorrow?" said Chloe.

"Uh, it already *is* tomorrow Chloe."

"Oh My God girl, you have got it bad!" she said.

Elle blushed, just thinking about Finn. She knew she had it bad. Finn was the first guy she had ever felt this deeply about. But what sucked the most, was his best friend was a douche bag. Tate had to go and screw everything up. Elle and I were supposed to be with either brothers or best friends...that had always been the plan, then Tate messed up. Now I'm sure Elle hated to admit she was happy...at least to me. I should have been madly in love with Tate, and making plans for college and the future with him. I know Elle feels like I jumped to conclusions about Tate. If she were honest with me, she thinks I should at least tell him why I'm so pissed and hear him out. She didn't know how he could talk his way out of that one, but the one plus is, as far as she knew, he had not been seeing Lisa since he started to see me. But, I was her best friend, and as long as I thought I was doing the right thing, she had to stand by me.

Elle looked at me "I'm just kidding, I promised I would call him that's all."

Just as we were about to get back in to my jeep, we saw a group of guys walking up to us. The gorgeous god was leading the pack. Oh shit, here goes. I started climbing in the jeep, desperately wishing the other girls would follow my lead. But, damn if they didn't close their doors back, and lean up against the side of the jeep. Come on now, aren't y'all as sleepy as I am, I thought. I don't have time for more guy drama.

"Ladies, where are y'all heading to so early?"

"Hey guys...didn't we see you all a couple of hours ago? Where did you run off too?" said Chloe.

Great Chloe, way to play it cool. We aren't supposed to even act like we remember them. I slumped down in my seat. Fine, I thought, y'all talk it out a for a couple of minutes then I'll start the car. That should be a sure fire sign that we were leaving.

"So, where are you heading to anyway," said the tall and thin one, talking directly to Maura?

"We're heading back to Elle's house on Emerald Isle." Oh thank God, Chloe was playing it smart for once. "We do have a pretty good drive ahead of us so I guess we better be taking off."

"Oh really, where at in Emerald Isle?"

Don't say it Chloe. We don't know anything about them, don't...

"Sailman's Pointe, you know the new development with the colored, beautiful houses." Shit, she said it. I laid my head back against the seat thinking I'd be hidden in the dark car until I heard...

"So what are you doing over here...hiding out?" the gorgeous god whispered in my open window. I think I jumped out of my skin.

"Oh my God...you scared me to death...I..um...I'm just really tired that's all." I could feel myself blushing. He really was pretty amazing to look at. And there's no telling what expression I had on my face when he snuck up on me.

"So, is your shoe still surviving? You were torturing it pretty good back there on the boardwalk," he said.

"Yes, my shoe's fine." I looked down at my feet, "thank you again for rescuing it."

"You look extremely fine in those heels, but may I suggest you wear flats around here next time?"

Well, if I wasn't blushing red before, I'm sure now I was scolding red and add speechless to the list. "I...um...what?"... fine, as in hot fine, or fine okay...then I said, "I mean, I'll wear whatever I damn well please."

Gorgeous god was stepping back a little holding his palms out in front of him. "Yes ma'am, I can see you sure would do that."

Crap, I had the bad habit of getting angry when I got embarrassed, and I had just exercised that little bad habit on him.

"Well, I guess you'd do good to remember that then." I said as I turned my head to the front away from him.

"Ooh, I like 'em feisty. Where have you been hiding Miss?"

Oh no you don't, we weren't even supposed to be talking this long. I just looked at him with a 'I'm not interested look'.

"Okay, I'll go first. My name is John....John Rider. Nice to meet you," he said holding his hand out.

My parents raised me to be polite, so it was like a knee-jerk reaction that I felt a need to shake his hand, with his waving around in the air in front of me.

"Reese Stanford." I said and then I turned the ignition on.

"Are you that much in a hurry to get out of here Reese? I mean, can't y'all stay for a little while longer? Where we are staying is uh very near here. How about y'all come over, and we can hang out a little?" Oh no you don't John. I have a boyfriend and I'm tired...well, I guess another knee jerk reaction...correction Reese, you had a boyfriend who turned out to be a little crazy, having an affair with my mother's friend...just thinking about that gave me chills up and down my spine.

"John, I appreciate the offer, really," I was trying to sound genuine. In fact it kind of was starting to be genuine. The longer he was standing in front of me for me to gape at I was beginning to wish I was staying. "But, we're exhausted. We had graduation this morning and …"

"Really, you just graduated from college? Us too..." he turned to look at the group of guys with him.

"No John, we just graduated from high school and are heading to college. Looks like you better keep searching for a group of more *mature* girls. You know we'd be entirely too naïve for your intellect."

"Whoa, someone's feeling a little insecure. I didn't say we still couldn't enjoy the company of some beautiful ladies just because you were a little younger, now did I?"

"You know, I think it would be best if you found college girls, that way we wouldn't crimp your style."

"Hey Reese, wait now, I think we've gotten off on the wrong foot. What's your story anyhow? Sounds like you've been burned by what you think are guys like me in the past"…

Now I was fuming. How dare he get so personal so quick. It was time to end this charade.

"Girls, it's time to go. I'm safe to drive, really...I only had one drink before dinner and even if that weren't the case, I would have just sobered up quickly." I looked at John to make sure he knew exactly what I meant.

After a few grumbles and sighs, everyone got in the car and we took off. The guys were standing around in a pack where our car once sat. I was so glad to be heading back to the house. I wanted to re-read Tate's text before I went to bed. And I wanted to have time to think about all that was going on in my head.

# CHAPTER 13

The next day we slept in until nearly 11am. We walked around in our fuzzy slippers, camisole and soft shorts, with our hair in a bun, on top of our head. It was safe to say we were dragging. There was a loud frog that had been croaking out the side of the house all night, making it hard to sleep. We made a pact to find the frog, and put it out of its misery, before we had another sleepless night. Yes, we were sleepy, but, you could still sense the excitement...our first day on the beach all year. Elle started running around getting the chairs and towels. Maura was fixing snacks and a cooler of Diet Dr. Pepper and water. Chloe was primping, and making sure her belly button ring matched her earrings. I of course was doing the only sensible thing, making a pitcher of lemonade and vodka. I mean, no need to drive and God knows I had enough sorrow to drown on the beach. First things first though, I wanted coffee! I had learned to drink it every morning this past year when I had to be at school early for student council meetings, and other committee meetings. Now it was a part of my every morning routine. Tate would sometimes bring me coffee before my meetings, even if he didn't have to be there that early at school himself. Ugh. He could be so sweet then.

I loved coffee midday too, if we were near a Starbucks. My friends weren't quite into coffee yet, so they mostly got the frozen drinks. I always got a grande non-fat, one pump of white mocha latte with light whip. I know...but it was a temporary glimpse at heaven each time I took that first sip. Wish we had a Starbucks close by. But, Elle's mom had a Keurig coffee maker at the house. Since I was the only one who drank coffee, it was easy to make me just one (sometimes two) piping hot cups of coffee. Hmmm. Now I was feeling more awake.

The sun felt amazing for the first part of June. You never can tell what North Carolina beaches are going to be like then. It could be cool and overcast or it could feel like the scorching summer came early, and be burning hot with no wind. Today though, it was neither. It was warm and there was a cool breeze blowing all around us.

We had just turned over on our stomachs...you know got to give even amount of time for each side. I mean, none of us wore less than 30 SPF, but we still like to get a little color for sure. We were listening to Humpty Hump, (a great party song from the 90's) and reading the most recent People, when I felt a cool drizzle of water running down my back. I jumped on my feet, momentarily dazed, then slowly realizing I had left my top lying on the chair below me. Although mortified, I was too shocked to move.

"Shit Reese, here..." Elle threw me my cover-up I had been using as a pillow under my chest.

Then it registered who was there...John...John and his group of guys.

"Damn Reese," John chuckled and looked mortified himself, "I guess I just lost more brownie points didn't I?"

"John, what the hell? You better believe it. What?...How did you know where to find us?" If I didn't look sunburned before, I knew now I was red all over from utter embarrassment...again.

"Well, it's not hard to find the most gorgeous group of girls on the planet, now is it? Besides, Emerald Isle is only so big, and there's only one Sailman's Pointe development."

I looked at Chloe like I could kill her... "Way to go Chloe. You would lead any serial killer right to our front door."

"Dang, that stung Reese." John said, as he covered his heart with his hand. "I promise you, those serial killing days are over," he laughed, "I've turned over a new leaf since then."

I punched him hard in the arm, so hard my hand hurt.

"Ouch, I'm just kidding, but I'll take any kind of touch you offer," he said with a wink.

I threw my water bottle at him.

John dodged it laughing hysterically. By now, everyone was laughing...

"I'm glad y'all find this funny. Some friends you are," I said looking around at my 'friends'.

I grabbed what was left of my dignity (along with my bikini top), and stomped off toward the beach house. I was so fed up with this...this boy shit. I didn't know which way to turn. I mean what was it? I wasn't deliberately asking for this attention. First Carter, then Tate, now John. All three gorgeous, fit guys. But each had his own story. Carter and Tate had let me down. I was sure John would too. I couldn't get inside fast enough. My friends weren't making any move to join me. I could only imagine they were enjoying the extra company. Well not me, I would be fine chilling and watching the soaps.

I had gotten a little too relaxed with the lemonade vodka and sunshine anyway.

Just as I was almost to the outside shower to rinse my feet off, I heard my name.

"Reese, wait up."

I thought, are you kidding me John? Ugh, can he just leave me alone? I am not interested!

I kept walking and went right inside the sliding glass door. And so did John.

"John, what in the world, did I invite you in?"

He jumped right back out with both feet on the deck, his whole body leaning in. "You're right, Reese. May I *please* come in?"

He looked so silly I just had to chuckle. His shoulders relaxed a little sensing I had lightened up.

"Reese, can I just have five minutes to talk with you? I mean, I did come all this way."

I almost blurted out – *I didn't ask you to.* I motioned my hand in the air like to say 'whatever'.

"So, is this your house?"

"Is this what you wanted to know? Are you looking for a real estate venture John?" I couldn't help it, I knew it was a smart ass remark, but I was in that kind of mood. I walked right inside the bathroom.

"Geez, put the claws back in Reese. I was just making small talk."

I was behind the locked bathroom door, trying to quickly retie my bathing suit and throw my cover up on, wondering what in the hell he was doing out there.

When I came back out, he was holding up a framed picture of Elle and me. We were probably around the age of twelve, our most awkward age. We were arm in arm, brown as ginger-bread girls, and mouths full of braces. Shit. I traipsed over to him and jerked it out of his hands.

"John what do you want?" He chuckled a little. God this man was exasperating, but so ridiculously gorgeous...ugh! I thought.

"I take it that was you?" he said with a smirk, "and it must have been Elle with you. You two were really cute Reese." I knew he was lying because we were hideously out of style.

"Look John, I'm not looking for a boyfriend okay, so I would suggest you don't waste your time..."

"Whoa, whoa Reese, wait...I mean no offense, but don't get ahead of yourself. I...uh...I just wanted to get to know you and spend a little time with you, that's all."

"Well, John, no offense to you either, but I've heard that a time or two and trust me, it didn't end well."

"Now I get it...you are talking like a woman that *has* been burned. What a shame Reese. When you do get a serious boy-friend again, the dude will have a lot to make up for." John had walked over to me, arms distance apart.

"Now you're already worried for my future boyfriend that you're so sure I'm going to have?"

John stepped a little closer to me. "Well, a guy has to watch out for himself doesn't he?"

"So now you're saying you *are* going to be my boyfriend, you are a confusing man John?"

"Well, since you asked so nicely?"

"JOHN!"

I threw my hands up in the air. "I give up," I said.

"No Reese, don't do that…I mean from where I stand that would be the worst thing you could do."

"You sound like my mom or Elle, not some guy I just met."

"Look, how about we go back down to the beach and hang out a while? I could stand to catch some rays." John said as he slipped back on his Maui Jim sunglasses.

"Oh, I guess I *should* stay with my friends," I said. "John, I'm not trying to be mean to you okay. I've just got a lot going on, and as long as you know where we stand from the beginning, I guess it wouldn't do any harm to lay out together as a group."

John let a slow, deep smile linger across his lips.

"Good," he said, "besides there would have been nothing to look forward to anyway, I already saw the goods," then he took off like he was going to run out the door before I hit him…again.

His remark about my topless moment on the beach made me gasp.

"John!"

"I'm just kidding Reese, just trying to lighten the mood."

He glanced over at me sideways as we were walking to the beach.

"I think you're just trying to be an ass."

He laughed out loud.

# CHAPTER 14

We hung out on the beach until nearly 5 pm. We had played corn hole, and football and jumping the waves for what felt like hours. For the most part they were a lot of fun. We even had hotdogs from the corner beachfront café. I had tried to keep my distance from John, but somehow he always found a way to be beside of me in the games we were playing.

John's friends seemed pretty cool. Brett was stocky and cute with short brown hair. He took up with Chloe right away. They seemed to hit it off. He was full of personality and himself for that matter. A little too wild if you ask me, but Chloe liked that sort of thing. Maura had seemed to be cozying up with Harrison. He was tall and slender with blondish hair and cute freckles to go with his dark tan. He evidently had just finished his bachelors in Science on his way to med school at UNC. Then there was Sam and Kerry. They too seemed pretty cool, but Elle didn't seem interested. She was just having a good time or at least trying to. She was completely smitten with Finn, so she wasn't getting too close to either.

We listened to Elle's iPod with speakers to all kinds of music on the beach. When "Single Ladies' by Beyonce came on, John and Brett jumped up and started singing to us...this without any drinking from them. They were hilarious. I couldn't believe they were that bold. We laughed so hard, watching them act like they were dancing on the stage. They were swinging their hips and snapping their wrists. They looked SO out of their element.

After the guys had surprised us, we only had water and soft drinks out of the cooler. I was amazed the guys hadn't brought any beer or alcohol. Maybe they really were more mature than most guys our age. Although, I would have been cool with a little beer...no biggie. Even my dad did that on the beach.

It had been a long day. I started getting together my beach bag and putting on my flip flops. I couldn't wait to go in for a long shower. I was sticky and my skin felt like sandpaper from playing in the ocean earlier.

"Hey, where are you going?" John had jogged up to me, and sat on the beach towel by my chair.

"Uh, going in...maybe you should too...that sunburn is going to feel pretty bad in a little while." I gently tapped my finger on his shoulder, turning the red to white under my touch. Crap, he was most likely going to make another comment about my 'touch'.

"You're probably right," he said. "Look, I was wondering if you and the girls wanted to come over for a little while this evening? We could grill out some shrimp or whitefish. We got lucky early this morning, and caught some off of Shackleford Banks."

"Shut up, you are kidding me. Y'all got up early enough to go fishing this morning and still felt like coming out on the beach?"

"Yeah, of course, I mean, that was our original reason for coming here together...to do a little salt water fishing."

"Oh really, it's not your reason any longer?" I said wondering why that just popped out of my mouth.

"Well, my reason just keeps evolving it seems." He looked at me with a sheepish grin.

Crap, I tried to change the subject real quick. "Um, I guess we're going to just stay here tonight..but I..."

"Hey, what are y'all talking about?" Chloe had walked up to us...looking so innocently curious...knowing damn well she had overheard the last part of our conversation.

"Nothing Chloe, just talking about how we were going to hang out here tonight..."

"Actually," John butted in "I was just inviting Reese and all of you over to our, uh, place..."

"What time?" Chloe blurted out.

"Chloe...I think maybe we should all talk about this." I eyed her like I was going to tear her head off.

"How about 8:00?" asked John. He was looking like he had just won the World Series (crap, Tate...why does something always have to make you pop in to my head...just thinking about baseball and there you are).

"We'll be there," said Maura casually holding Harrison's hand.

"Well wonderful," I said sarcastically. "I guess I'm outnumbered unless, Elle, what do you think?"

Elle glanced up at me with a carefree look. "I think it would be good for you, I mean us to have a little fun."

John quickly looked over at me as if to say, I heard that. Luckily he didn't comment.

"So where is your house John?" asked Elle.

"Well, basically where you were last night?"

"You mean at Beaufort?"

"Yeah…how about if we meet you at the Dock Side restaurant, then we can walk you to it…We'll get everything we need for dinner. Y'all can get it next time," he said with a wink.

Dang, he is presumptuous, I'll give him that.

"Okay, that will work. We'll see you at 8:00. Here is my number," said Chloe "in case you think of something we can bring.

We all said goodbye and headed up to the house. Chloe had a new aura of excitement about her as did Maura. Elle was just ready to get to the phone, and call Finn. I however, seemed more lost than ever.

What was I doing? I should be jumping at the chance to move on from Tate. I had spoken to my mom, and learned that Tate had gone on to Myrtle Beach with his friends after graduation (at least that's what she had read on Facebook …Tate's Mom was one of her 'friends' on there). He'd originally planned not to go, but I guess he changed his mind after we broke up. I had all sorts of crazy thoughts of how he was meeting a different girl a day and enjoying his freedom. That should have been fueling my fire enough to let my hair down as well, but I just wasn't into it.

I laid my head back on the sofa, and drifted off to sleep, until my phone pinged.

> I enjoyed today Reese.
>
> Looking forward to this evening.
>
> In case you're wondering, I'm not a stalker… Chloe shared your #
>
> with me. — John

Ugh…Chloe I am truly going to kill you, I said under my breath. Luckily she was already in the shower, or I would've tried.

I did have a small smile creep up my face. No sooner did John pop in to my head did my phone ping again.

> Reese I think of you always.
>
> I am still missing you
>
> I wish I could see you. Please text
>
> me back. – Tate

What in the hell Tate. Ahhh…Is that supposed to be some kind of sign God? I don't get it. Why doesn't he just give up already…Maybe he really does care about me?

The more I thought about all of Tate's texts, and the fact that he may not be enjoying himself as much as I thought, I was getting a little upset about how I had handled things. Maybe I should talk with him about what I knew. Maybe I should give him a chance to offer an explanation.

I took a shower and dried off, wondering the whole time if I should even go to John's place. I mean that was a little crazy to go over to someone's house I'd just met, even if I was with my friends. I had my hair wrapped up in a towel about to head to Elle's room and tell her I had changed my mind, when my phone pinged again.

> Reese, I am back at home finally.
>
> My rehab is going well
>
> I REALLY miss you, but hope you are having fun.

Sorry again I had to tell you about

Tate like I did,

My mom says you broke up with him.

BTW, she doesn't know you know about her.

Hey, I saw pictures of Tate on Facebook at Myrtle Beach with lots of girls,

So I'm guessing he's okay.

Let's catch up when you get home... Carter

I had to read his book of a text three times before it sunk in what he was saying. Tate was being wild at Myrtle Beach. That meant girls, and funneling beer I'm sure (because that was unfortunately a staple if you were at MB for senior week). Those two together were a disaster for the best of guys. And how in the world does Lisa know we broke up. Tate? No, hopefully it was my mom. I decided to call my mom and ask her if she had told Carter's mom.

"Hey Mom."

"Oh hey honey. How's it going?"

"We're brown already," I said with a half laugh.

"Wear sunscreen! I've told you that you don't want to look too old too soon."

I cut her off "Mom, I know. Listen, I've been meaning to ask you if you told anyone about Tate and me breaking up?"

"Well, I did talk with your dad about it. He wasn't sure what was going on as I wasn't either. He just assumed it was the fight between Tate and Carter."

"So you didn't tell anyone else?"

"Well, Lisa and I were talking about it and she secretly hopes you get back with Carter. She said he really misses you."

"Mom, please don't talk about me and Tate with Lisa." Oh shoot, I didn't want to sound too strange about it. "I mean, whatever happens with me and Tate could just upset Carter, you know."

"I guess you're right honey. It's just Lisa is a close friend and she's just as worried about you as I am."

"Mom, speaking of Lisa, we never really talked about her and Tony's issues. Since they were back together I was hoping you would fill me in. You know, to help me understand Carter's circumstances a little better."

"You're right honey. I should've already talked with you about this, given your history with Carter and all. Well, I guess you know Lisa and Tony had separated because she, um, well she was seeing someone else and Tony found out."

"Mom did you know she was doing that?" I asked completely shocked at how nonchalant she was acting.

"No way sweetheart. I wouldn't have supported it. I'm just here for the aftermath. She tried her best to make me understand, she had turned to someone else because of the way Tony had been to her…she says he was somewhat abusive. But now Reese, we don't know what was happening in their house, so don't think badly of Tony yet. He's still a friend of your fathers."

"I can't imagine Dad would still be his friend if he was like that…you know, hurting Lisa, physically."

"We saw some bruises on her over the years, but she always had an explanation for them like…gardening, working out, falling and so on. So until they broke up we had no idea.

Your dad, not knowing 100% either way, is just here for them now, to help mend their marriage. The fact that they both are willing to try is a start I guess."

"Mom, do you know who she was seeing that broke them up?"

"No honey, I don't. That's one thing she won't share with me. She said I wouldn't understand. And, she's right about that, I don't understand cheating at all."

"Okay Mom. Well, I better get going. We're going to get something to eat. Love you."

I felt bad about not telling her how we were going to get something to eat with some guys we had just met. But, it would be fine. I just kept thinking back to Carter's text.

Any thoughts I had before about skipping tonight went out the window. I quickly got ready, making sure I was as done up as I could get. I curled my hair so it hung in long locks beyond my shoulders, slipping in a little diamond hairpin to lift it off my left cheek (Tate always loved that...said it made access to my neck easier and helped my perfume to linger). The diamond pin was my grandmother's and I always felt like it brought me luck. I also wore my birthday Versace perfume (Carter had given me before he left last year). And of course, I wore wedge pumps to accentuate my long legs and calves. I slipped on the J Crew dress my mom had gotten me with the other 'graduation clothes shopping trip' we had. I made my lashes extra curly and long by heating up my eyelash curler with the hairdryer, and swiping a layer of mascara on the tips. Then I applied blush and clear gloss to my already red from the sun lips. I was ready....for what I wasn't sure, but ready none the less.

As I walked out of the bathroom, I heard cat calls all around from my friends. They looked gorgeous, but were shocked to see that I had gone to such lengths to try and look that way too. "What?" I screeched. "I just decided to get dressed up a little." I said as I twirled around.

"Bitch. It's not like you don't get noticed enough." Chloe said as she walked up and grabbed both of my hands leaning back to give me the once over. Then she hugged me. "It's about time you came to life. John will shit himself."

"Wait, that is *not* what I'm trying to do Chloe."

"Well you should have thought about that before you came out dressed like a Vanity Fair shoot," then she laughed. "I'm joking Reese, but you should see your face."

"Ok girls, lets hit the road," said Elle looking awesome in her yellow, slinky spaghetti strap dress. The color made her blue eyes pop. Maura was dressed so beautiful too in her coral sun dress and turquoise wedges. She was sure to make an impression with Harrison. Chloe had on a pink sundress and navy wedges. Her long, thick, brown hair stick straight, and half-way down her back. Chloe was amazingly gorgeous, she just didn't see it. She had true self-esteem issues. That was a topic for another time, for sure.

"Let me grab my water bottle," I said as I winked at Elle. It was pink with a slide lid. I didn't go anywhere where drinking was happening without it.

We drove with the top up to my jeep so we wouldn't mess up our well-primped hair. We were riding down the road giggling about this or that, when all of a sudden Maura screamed. I nearly jumped out of my skin and Elle swerved the car, almost running off the road. "Oh shit, oh shit," Maura said, her hand stretched out in front of her pointing at the dash. It was a frog…the tiny green frog that had kept us up half the night with a croak that was louder than an alarm. Well probably not the exact same one, but possibly. His beady eyes were staring right at her. We were all cracking up at how scared Maura was and were laughing so hard, our sides hurt. She was screaming at us to pull over and get it out. All of a sudden, it jumped, no, it flew off the dash onto Maura's shoulder. She was thrashing about yelling for us to get it off. Now we were screaming too. It was funny, but I really didn't want that thing jumping on me either. Elle was barely able to pull safely off on the side of the busy highway, and all four doors opened at once trying to shoo this frog out. What a sight we were, I was still laughing hysterically when the frog finally jumped out causing Maura to scream one last time. Whew, I was exhausted from laughing so hard, but it felt SO good to laugh like that. "What else could happen tonight girls?" Maura asked after she got buckled back in. "Huh, and y'all were laughing at me. Well, have a killer frog attack you and you won't be laughing so hard…" Then she too burst out laughing. We talked and laughed about it the rest of the way.

We got to the DockSide about 8:15 pm (better to make the boys wait). I had a Bud Lite on the way there. I really didn't like beer, but it was easy and we had a case in our refrigerator. Thankfully, it did relax me a little. We each made a vow to take care of each other and never drink an open drink we hadn't had our eyes on the whole time. The media was enough to scare everyone about date rape, without having to discuss my own personal trauma, so everyone agreed.

We were walking up to the waterfront, wondering how far their place was when we saw the guys. They looked great, of course. They were in khakis and blue jeans. John had on a v-neck tight, black t-shirt and faded blue jeans. He was looking hot for sure. His eyes lit up when he saw me. He actually looked a little nervous all of a sudden.

"Ladies you are looking divine," said Brett. He walked up to Chloe kissing her square on the lips. She looked over at me and shrugged her shoulders.

I stood back a ways from everyone, feeling a little uncomfortable from all of the attention we were getting. Not just from our new friends, but from other's around the boardwalk.

John came up to me, "Reese you look absolutely amazing, I mean wow…I…wow."

Why was I blushing?…Oh no, I didn't want him so see me blushing.

He leaned in and whispered, "And that blushing makes you look that much more divine. What I would do to know what you were thinking." He kissed my cheek.

"John, please…"

"I'm sorry, I just can't help myself. I can't take my eyes off of you. Please don't be mad."

"Just try to contain yourself John…seriously." I said with a light-hearted chuckle hoping I didn't come across too cocky.

He reached for my hand. I reluctantly took his. He gave me a sideways grin of yet another win for him. I felt guilty… actually felt guilty…Why? I sighed. I will have to admit, his skin against mine did feel really good.

"So, how far is your place John?" asked Maura.

"Just a few steps North and a couple of steps West," he said with a huge grin on his face.

"What? I don't get it. I said. How could that…" I quickly realized we were walking in between the boats. I mean the YACHTS at the private docks. We stopped directly in front of a monster of a ship called 'J Rider III'. "John, are you a III?" I asked trying to hide my shock, thinking this must be someone else's boat.

"I'm afraid so," he said, his hand still encasing mine.

The other girls were jumping up and down, giggling.

"It was my graduation gift from my Grandfather last month. He gives somewhat extravagant gifts I guess."

"You think? What on earth? I mean who our age, I mean your age (knowing he was four years older than me) has a yacht?"

"Probably some form of a write off for the company if I know my Granddad."

"Wait," said Maura. "I recently read a story about Rider Industries. Are *you the* Rider Industries that owns oil plants in several countries, including here?"

"That would be my family, the Riders. I'm supposed to be groomed to fall into suit as well. I guess this gift was just another assurance from my Grandfather and Father that it would actually happen."

"Whoa Reese. You better scoop him up. Forget about Tate, and Carter too for that matter," said Chloe.

Holy shit. Did she just say that out loud? I turned to her, mortified.

"Chloe, shut up." If my eyes could shoot lasers, I would have just annihilated her.

John just gave a quick squeeze of my hand, and a quick glance as if to say what, that it was okay? Or that we would discuss that later? I wasn't sure, but I was going to have to talk with Chloe later about her big mouth and how to learn to rein it in. Elle just looked at me with an 'I'm sorry' look and gave a little shrug.

"Come on ladies. Why don't you take a look around? Guys, let's go get a drink for them and get the food on."

As soon as they left we were giggling like crazy. We were barely able to hold our excitement. How rich John, hell maybe all of them had to be.

"Reese, if you go acting all goody two shoes and screw this up for us, so help me I will throw you overboard." Then she jumped up and down clapping her hands together. "This just might very well be the time of our lives."

"Are you kidding me Chloe...I could so kill you right now. Please watch what comes out of your mouth...okay?"

"I'm only trying to help out," she said "you'll be thanking me tomorrow, you wait and see."

Maybe so...but why did I feel so strange about what was happening. Maybe it had something to do with the fact that we were on a yacht worth, I don't know, millions? Maybe, because we had just met these guys yesterday for crying out loud. Or, maybe because we really should have let our parents or someone know where we were...just in case. Damn Reese stop being so crazy...Ugh...but I couldn't seem to ease the knots in my stomach.

We would have to stay with each other at all times...that I knew for sure.

# CHAPTER 15

The ship was absolutely amazing. It had all the bells and whistles: two large bedrooms, two bathrooms, a dining area with a full size stainless steel refrigerator, a wet bar, 3 decks (one just for sunbathing), a captain and a full-time ship attendant. How could anyone have this much money? What was strange and good I guess, is so far John hadn't acted like he was that wealthy. We were gaping at every little detail, barely able to take it all in; standing over at the railing looking into the dark, black water below…the moon was brightly reflecting off the sea.

When, all of a sudden I felt hands come up to gently grab my waist. I gave a soft squeal and jumped.

"John, you scared me to death! I can't believe all of this is yours." I said breathless from the fact that I had just about jumped out of my skin, again with him.

"You okay?" he said chuckling, noticing how my breathing had changed. He smirked up at me with sensual eyes…seemingly aroused by my breathiness. Good grief, I thought.

"Yeah sure, just a little jumpy I guess."

"No need to worry Reese, I won't bite," he said as he gave me a little wink.

John was just so dang gorgeous. His teeth were bright white and perfectly straight, accentuated by the tan color of his skin. You could tell he had been very well groomed throughout his younger years. And his blue eyes were simply piercing.

"Hey," he said gently turning me towards him (I sheepishly looked around for all of my friends who were still gazing over the railing). "I know I've already told you, but you look absolutely amazing. I can't get over how beautiful you are. There is something about you Reese. I can't quite put my finger on it… an innocence maybe? I'm not sure."

Innocence? Oh God, I wish that were the case. Unfortunately it was taken from me a while ago. I looked down at my feet and silently shifted a little from side to side.

He softly lifted my chin so my eyes would be looking directly in his.

"Reese, I don't want you to feel uncomfortable, but I'm looking forward to getting to know you a little better."

I looked around again at my friends who were now talking to the other guys. At least everyone was present and accounted for I thought. This is usually Maura's job, to keep things organized like a mother hen, but when it came to guys, I couldn't be cautious enough.

He gently pulled my eyes back to him. I enjoyed looking at him, that was for sure.

"John, I think it would be nice to spend some time together, all of us…" "But?…" he said feeling like I maybe had something coming behind that.

"*But*, I really am not looking for a relationship of any kind right now. Not to mention I am only here for a little while at the beach, then it's back to reality."

"Listen Reese, all I'm asking for is some time to get to know you a little better...who knows, we could be pen pals after this," he said chuckling.

I chuckled too, "that would be cute...us expecting a letter from each other, snail mail weekly."

John got serious all of a sudden. "Reese, who are Tate and Carter?"

I sighed a little, shifting my gaze around. "I can't believe you remember their names after one comment from Chloe."

"I don't think I will quickly forget anything that has to do with you," he said.

That was sweet, and a little forward, but it helped me open up a little.

"Well, Tate was my boyfriend of nearly a year until a little over two weeks ago, and Carter was my boyfriend for six months before Tate."

"Oh, so you have had some pretty serious relationships," he said keeping his eyes on mine. "How could I think any different, I'm sure guys have been lined up for a chance at your attention."

"Hmmm...let's just say I'm used to guys letting me down." I can't believe I was even talking about Tate and Carter with him. "John, I came here to get away from all of that, so can we not talk about them anymore, please?"

"Of course Reese...I just feel like I need to go kick their ass or something for letting you down. I just hope you don't think all guys are like that."

"No offense John, but yeah, I actually do think all guys are like that." I winced and John put his hand over his heart like he had just been shot. I let out a soft laugh. "I'm sorry but it's true. That's why I'm not the best girl for you to be wasting your time on. I'm sure there are lots of other girls dying for you to be taking them on a tour of your yacht." I silently wondered how often that actually happened for him.

Like he could read my mind he said "well, I don't typically bring girls up here. Yeah, the guys always want to, but I'm a pretty private person Reese."

"Is that so? Well shyness is certainly not a virtue of yours now is it?" I motioned to his hands still placed around my waist. I realized I was leaning back a bit from his face feeling a little too close for comfort.

He dropped his hands and stepped in a bit towards me. I was suddenly flushed, I could feel the heat rising up my neck.

"Would you mind if I gave you a kiss Reese? I mean being this close to you with the setting of the boat swaying and moonlight on the water. Me standing *this* close to a beautiful girl seems like it belongs in a movie."

"Oh my, that must be a line you've used a time or two, you have it down pat...and I hate to tell you but this is *not* a movie John."

"Oh, I beg to differ Reese. I haven't EVER used those words on a girl before, and I think we would make a great movie." He laughed when he saw my eyes get big. "You know what I mean, a romance or chick flick?" He quickly recovered.

He got serious again and whispered near my face.

"And you didn't answer my question Reese, can I please kiss you?"

I stared at him for a moment, evidently a little too long because he leaned in slowly, his fingers gently holding my chin up a little...oh my, is this really happening? Then with the softest lips, he touched his to mine. Mine instinctively parted a little, which made him give out a slow breath, sending chills down my back. His body was almost leaning on mine.

The kiss felt like it lasted for minutes, but he swiftly pulled back. My eyes stayed closed for a few beats longer...my heart racing.

"Now that was made for movies," he said.

My eyes were blinking but I still hadn't moved.

Before he could say anything else, Elle cleared her throat and casually walked up to us.

"Hey guys," she eyed me almost wickedly "we're getting hungry around here."

John smiled at me, that gorgeous smile, "Absolutely, dinner, coming right up." He held my eyes a beat longer, then he jogged to the dining area, like he had a new burst of energy. We could smell food grilling. Music was playing around the ship on outdoor and indoor speakers. Jason Mraz's voice belting out his smooth lyrics.

Elle had my drink in her hand. Handing it to me she said "I saw the attendant open a new bottle of vodka and poor it in, with a real splash of lime, cranberries and a new bottle of tonic water. You are good to go Reese."

"Thanks Elle." She watched as I poured it into the pink water bottle I had set down earlier. It was transparent, so I could tell nothing was in it before I put my own drink in it. You never could be too careful.

"What was that kiss Reese? I mean that was kind of quick don't you think? I felt a need to interrupt. He is ridiculously handsome and rich, but his body was all but smashing up against yours."

I wanted to tell her how he said it was because I was so beautiful, but even I knew how lame that sounded.

"I know Elle. I'm glad you came over when you did. I'm a little weak right now I guess." I told her about the text I had gotten from Carter, and what my mom had said.

"Oh Reese, I can see why you want to show you can have fun too, just be careful, not only physically, but also with your feelings." She threw her arm over my shoulders.

"You're right. Hey, let's all make sure we keep on top of things tonight. I just have a strange feeling about being on this boat."

# CHAPTER 16

We were having a *really* great time. Dinner was delicious. The guys seemed extra proud we were enjoying their catch of the day. The night air was amazing. Us girls were dancing on the deck, giggling and just being happy to be together. We were drinking a little of course, except for Elle. She was still having a good time though. You could tell because she was grinning and out of breath from dancing.

I was actually feeling really relaxed, and ambitious to show off a few dance moves (which without a little alcohol, would not be happening in front of them),...when John came up behind me and starting moving with me.

At first my body's reaction was to stiffen up and slow down, but when I looked back at his face, he seemed to have a cute, innocent, fun-loving expression. I couldn't help but to turn around and chuckle at him.

"What? I have a few moves myself," he said as he crossed his feet and quickly did a turn then bowed. We both laughed out loud.

"That kind of looked like a Michael Jackson move, not a John Rider one," I said. But, just by the way he was moving, I could tell he had rhythm.

Then a slow song came on and he sweetly held out his hand and asked me to dance. I of course said I would oblige him. He gently took me into a close embrace as we ever so lightly swayed.

"I have enjoyed you being here this evening Reese. I don't want to scare you off, but I was watching you dance earlier, I can't seem to take my eyes off of you tonight."

"Well then, that is a problem, considering we've been here for over four hours. You must need to at least rest your eyes by now."

"Ha, ha...I could go all night and tomorrow, and not need to rest from looking at you," he whispered.

I was keeping a check on all the girls around the deck, making sure everyone was okay. John, however, was being very distracting. I couldn't locate Chloe until my eyes swept the other end of the boat. She was talking with Brett, their heads together. I was hoping she was watching how much she had to drink, and was keeping her head on straight. As I brought my eyes back to where they were, they stopped halfway when I spotted Sam. He was staring at me with a dark look on his face. Worried he had caught me looking, I quickly reverted my eyes back to John. For some reason, I felt like Sam had been staring at me more than once like that tonight.

"So, how long have you known all of your friends John? Did y'all meet in college?"

"Harrison and Sam grew up with me in Charlotte. But, I didn't meet Brett and Kerry until college. So I guess you could say we've been close friends for a while now."

"Do their families come from money too?" I cringed, I didn't mean for it to come out like that. "I mean do they have mega companies as well?"

He chuckled "actually, Sam's Dad and my Dad are sort of partners. So, I guess you could say he does in a sense, but Harrison's parents are in medicine, Brett's dad is a stock broker, and Kerry's dad is a lawyer."

"Oh really? Tate, I mean my ex-boyfriends' parents are lawyers."

John sighed a little. "So, now I get to hear about the infamous Tate. What is your story with him Reese…if you don't mind me asking?"

I actually did mind him asking, but I was feeling so relaxed, I was more willing to answer. "We dated and now we don't… the truth is, I was in love with him, and he, he wasn't who I thought he was."

"Oh…and you're not going to elaborate are you?" John asked. I shook my head and bit my lower lip. "And Carter, are you still in love with him?"

"Wow, you are not embarrassed to ask the tough questions right off are you?" I said feeling a little exposed. "Well, I thought I had been in love with him, but regret is what I mostly feel now. Regret, because he broke my heart and I didn't get over him quick enough, I guess. I was still hanging on a bit even while I was dating Tate. But I didn't realize it then. Oh my, I have no idea why I just told you all of that John. I mean that is SO unlike me. I don't know what came,"

Before I could finish, I felt his soft lips swiftly cover mine. This time his tongue quickly followed, touching gingerly to mine, then with more force. He took a sharp intake of breath, as did I, and we were kissing. His right hand that had been around my waist slowly started moving up my left arm, and then back down again, like he was caressing me. It really did start to affect me, and I let a little moan slip from my lips. Oh shit, I was really starting to get light-headed. We moved slowly over to the side rail. He would pull his lips from mine and look at me, then gingerly place them back on me. Then he started trailing kisses down my neck. Oh my God, I thought. I shouldn't be doing this, but oh it feels so good. Then he pulled his lips back to mine, somehow even more sensual than before. I could feel my body responding all over, tingling and getting heated.

I ever so slowly pushed him back, his lips were the last thing to disconnect from me. "John," I said completely out of breath. "Let's not get carried away. I think we have had too much to drink, especially after such a long day." Wow, if John was really this sweet and sensual, I wondered how fast I would fall for him. That thought alone was freaking me out. Surely, his true colors would show soon. He was too good to be true. I was NOT going to be hurt by a man again.

I stepped back a little and slowly looked around the room trying to regain my composure. I saw Elle and Maura, they were both still dancing. But, Chloe was nowhere to be seen. "I actually need to use the rest room. I'm definitely not used to having vodka tonics." I gave a somewhat uncomfortable chuckle.

"By all means Reese, do you remember where it is? Last door on the left down these stairs. I'll go up a deck and check out the snacks we have. It's been a while since you ate. If you're not used to drinking this much, we better get some food on your stomach. I can't have you getting sick. I mean, I was hoping we could hang out on the beach again tomorrow. But, I'm sure you wouldn't want to if you're feeling like crap," he laughed a little, reaching up and caressing my face.

I smiled...feeling very happy about my emotions at the moment. I tiptoed down the stairs unsure of where the others were. Not seeing anyone, I walked towards the bathroom, but before I could get to the door, I felt rough hands grab my arm and pull me into one of the bedrooms.

I was slammed against the wall and a hand thrown over my mouth. It was Sam! What was he doing? I tried to holler his name through his hand, but the sound was muffled. His eyes were still dark, but his pupils were severely dilated. He looked evil...even un-human like.

"You've been teasing me all night Reese. I see you looking at me. You want me, don't you Reese, Huh?" He shoved his body against mine his hand still over my mouth. My eyes wide and worried. I froze at first, then I tried to fight him off with my hands. He quickly grabbed both of my hands and threw them against the wall above my head, holding them there.

"Don't scream Reese, or I might just have to break your neck." He laughed. "Besides the guys already know what's happening down here," he said.

Please God, tell me they didn't know he would do this, is all I could think.

I couldn't move. The fear had to be apparent in my eyes. Tears started streaming down my face. "Oh, you want me to be in you already Reese, is that why you're crying? Well don't worry my teasing bitch, I'm about to honor your wish."

Oh God, help me. Somebody please come down here. Elle, please come looking for me. I can't go through this again. I'd rather die. My eyes pleaded with Sam. I tried again to scream but no sound came out from his hand. I felt like I was suffocating.

He pulled up my dress exposing my panties. "Oh" he said with a growl "you even wore a thong just for me. Well, maybe it was meant for John at first, until you discovered how much you wanted me."

He was talking deranged, like he was a different person. I couldn't fathom to think what I was going to feel next. He ran his hand up and down my abdomen, then roughly cupped my sex. He reached around with his loose hand and grabbed me so hard I was sure he would leave a huge bruise. I was worried that wasn't all he would leave me with. He reached down to my thigh and shoved my legs apart, hard squeezing the inside of my right thigh as he hissed "my how ready you are."

God, why is this happening again? Please help me before it is too late. I hadn't talked to God in so long, I knew it was dis-respectful just to be begging Him now to help me, but I truly needed Him to come through. I shut my eyes tight continuing to pray and cry. Then I kneed Sam hard in the groin. He cussed and squeezed my hands tighter, then with his other hand he hit me hard in the face. My left eye felt like it had been blown out. I could barely see out of it. Then he got close to me and trying to kiss me he said, "I'll do it again. Be still."

I thought I was going to throw up right there. And I closed my eyes trying to figure out what to do.

Sam snapped at me "Open your eyes Reese. I want you to look at me while I take you." He tried pulling down my panties, but he was having difficulty, so he ripped them off. Then he started undoing his jeans. He was about to lunge towards me when the door flung open.

It was John.

He jumped on Sam and they started fighting. John hollered for me to find Elle. I didn't wait for him to say it again, I took off. I ran up the stairs as fast as I could, although it was so hard...my legs felt like jelly and I was about to pass out. Whatever buzz I had was long gone.

I was frantically searching for Elle and the girls, when I heard loud noises coming from a door near the top of the stairs. It was cracked open so I quickly pushed it in.

"Oh my God, Chloe..."

Chloe was throwing up in a trashcan and Maura was holding her hair. Over to her right side was what looked like white powder on a mirror and a short straw. It registered then what I was seeing. Cocaine! That's what was wrong with Sam, drugs! He was high and out of control.

I kneeled down to Chloe, "No, no tell me you didn't do this Chloe. We have to get out of here. I knew this was crazy coming here."

Maura looked at my face and bruises on my wrists and gasped.

"Sam attacked me Maura, he tried to rape me. We have to go now!"

"Chloe can't walk out of here Reese, what do we do? None of us can carry her. She's dead weight."

Brett was passed out in the chair near the corner...probably from drugs too.

"Get John," she said.

"I'm sorry Maura, but I don't trust *any* of them. Let's drag her out of here."

Elle finally came running down the stairs and screamed when she saw me.

113

I grabbed both of her hands willing her to listen to me.

"Elle, I have to leave, I can't stay here but we can't carry Chloe out. Since you're sober, take this pepper spray and these keys...guard these two," I said pointing to Maura and Chloe. "And drive home as soon as she can walk. Tell these guys you will call the police if they come even one step close to you."

I knew that sounded so irrational, and I was only hoping I was leaving my friends in a safe way, but I ran as fast as I could off of the yacht. I had no idea what was happening between John and Sam. In fact, I didn't know where the captain or Kerry and Harrison were. It was all so strange. I just knew I had to flee. There happened to be a cab waiting outside the row of restaurants. I flagged him over and told him the directions to Elle's beach house. I wasn't thinking clearly, this I knew, but nothing else was making sense. My cell phone was dead so I couldn't even keep track of what was happening with the girls. I was scared out of my mind.

Do I call the police? I was afraid to do that until they were able to get Chloe out of there. If she had done cocaine, she would be arrested. I couldn't stand to think of her with that record.

Oh Chloe, why did you have to do it? Were you that drunk? We've NEVER touched drugs before, and in one night you lose yourself.

I knew all too well what one night could do. The only difference was I didn't choose to lose myself, someone had chosen for me.

My body was still trembling all over. I faintly heard the cab driver ask if he could take me to the hospital, and I was barely able to shake my head no.

Thirty minutes and lots of praying later (after all, I felt like I was rescued just in the nick of time…was that God?…I had to think it was) I was getting out at the beach house and was able to shakily pay the driver.

I hunted desperately for the key under the giant seashell in the landscaping, and after dropping it twice, I finally managed to unlock the door.

I'd looked around in my purse for my phone but I couldn't find it anywhere. I ran outside searching the ground for it. I must have left it on the cab seat. I vaguely remember sitting it down. I don't even know what cab company I used. It was all a fog now. I screamed and fell to the ground pounding my fist on the grass.

Elle's parents had taken out the house phone last year, since everyone had cell phones. I guess one less bill a month or something like that.

I had no way to get in touch with any of them. I slowly stumbled back to the bathroom and looked at myself in the mirror. I couldn't recognize the battered girl staring back at me. My right eye was black and blue and nearly closed from the swelling.

I sunk down to the floor, covering my hands with my face. I was lost, my soul completely dark, without a shred of light. I was rocking back and forth each time feeling the bruises on my back and thighs.

Somehow, I must have drifted off to sleep in a fetal position. I woke up to loud banging. I knew if it were Elle she would use her key. Oh my God, what if it was Sam? I backed up in to the bathroom corner as far as I could, curling in to as tight of a ball as I could get. Again, I was praying intensely, praying that I would be spared.

I heard a glass break and what must have been the front door being flung against the wall. I couldn't breathe. Who was there?

I was afraid any noise, even a breath, would alert whoever the perpetrator was where I was hiding. Not moving a muscle, I waited for my pending doom.

Then I heard it, the all too familiar voice. "Reese, oh my God, Reese are you here?"

Another male voice said "there's her purse, she must be here."

The first voice said "you go upstairs and I'll look down here."

Even though the voice was familiar, I was still unsure and scared to death. Barely breathing I watched the bathroom door. Praying they wouldn't open it and just leave. No quicker than I could think it, the door flung open and I screamed.

"Oh Reese…" then he yelled "she's in here!"

# CHAPTER 17

couldn't see straight, adrenaline had flooded into my veins and before I could recognize who had rushed in the door, I had passed out.

I woke up lying on the couch, covered in a blanket. I could feel someone sitting beside of me, because the couch was heavily indented to the side. I felt a cool, wet washcloth on my forehead.

But as my mind started clearing, I started to scramble, trying to sit up and get away from whoever was there.

"Shhh Reese, it's okay now."

I knew that voice immediately. My eyes met his.

"Tate!"

I was barely able to whisper his name, but saying it made my heart hurt. I couldn't believe he was here. He grabbed me up in a hug and I winced. But I had never seen anyone or anything more beautiful in all my life.

"Tate you're here...how did you know?" I croaked, barely able to speak.

"Elle. She called us..." his voice got strange like he was trying to control his emotions, and keep from crying.

"Us?" I glanced around slowly and my eyes caught up with Finn's.

"Hi Reese, you scared us to death. How are you feeling?"

"I um…Oh God, where are they…Elle, and the girls…they were still there." I tried getting up again but Tate put his arms around me.

"I just got a call from them," said Finn. "I was on my way to get them when Elle said they were leaving. They should be walking in the door any second. Elle filled us in, so don't try to talk now, just rest. Tate wasn't about to leave you."

I didn't know what to say, so I looked at Tate. His eyes were sweetly set on mine. "How did y'all get here so fast?" I said.

"We were at Myrtle Beach, which is only about three hours from here. With Finn driving, we made it in a little over two."

"Man, it didn't hurt that you threatened to kill me if I didn't get you to Reese quick!" Finn said.

I looked up at Tate. "Well thank you both…" then I remembered why I ended up there at John's in the first place…the Facebook pictures of Tate. Now wasn't the time to discuss those.

No sooner could I think of what to say next, the front door swung open.

"Reese!"

"She's awake and she's doing okay. A little beat up though." I caught Tate's eyes as he seethed the last part from his teeth.

"What in the world Reese," said Elle, "I've called you a hundred times. Why didn't you answer?"

"I can't find my phone. I must have left it in the cab when I pulled it out to call you. My battery was dead and so I thought

I put it back in my purse. I can't even remember what cab company brought me here."

"Don't worry, there's only one company that goes to Beaufort. We'll find it," said Maura.

I looked around Maura for Chloe. I was so angry at her, but I also was relieved when I finally saw her beautiful face. "Don't say anything Reese," she whimpered. "Elle, Maura, and John have already beat me up enough." She cringed when she said that, knowing I was the one that had been physically beaten up.

They all walked over to me and hugged me. Chloe was last. "I'm sorry Reese. I love you, and we could've all gone home together, if I hadn't been such a damn weakling and tried, well, you know. I guess I was overcome with everything; the money...everything...I'm sorry." She was sobbing and begging my forgiveness with her eyes on mine.

I hugged her back. "Chloe, I'm still furious. You went back on our promise for us to watch out for each other, instead you were breaking another promise and getting high. Tell me you won't ever touch that stuff again."

"Oh Reese," she sobbed into my neck "I promise... I can't stand to see you like this. What that bastard could have done to you," cried Chloe.

"I'm afraid to ask, but what happened to Sam and John?" I said.

"I'll tell you what *will* happen to them," fumed Tate. "I'm going to kill them."

I put my hand on Tate's wrist. "Let's all calm down. I want to kill Sam myself." I said seriously but with a chide chuckle.

"John beat the shit out of Sam, but not without Sam probably cracking a rib or two of John's," Elle said.

"Who are these guys? They sound like real winners that y'all came across ladies...I thought y'all knew better than that," said Finn, looking right at Elle.

She flushed. "We met them the night before at Beaufort on the boardwalk. Then they 'found' us on the beach the next day and Chloe quickly agreed for us all to have dinner at their place last night...We had no idea their *place* would be an enormous yacht, or that they would be in to drugs."

"I'm sorry guys. It was a bad idea...you know I don't think straight at times," said Chloe putting her head down.

"We all got carried away," I said. "I thought they were good too...obviously, looks can be deceiving." I glanced up at Tate as I said those words. I started to get up, but felt a little woozy. Tate reached out and grabbed my hand. I reluctantly let him have it while Carter's text was popping back in my head.

"Let me help you Reese. I'll walk with you," he said.

As soon as I stood up, I felt a breeze under my dress, and sudden warmth from the blush rising up my neck. "Tate, did you find me this morning in the bathroom?" Oh crap, I thought, I hope my dress was down when he found me.

"I did, you had just passed out onto the floor," said Tate.

"I realize I, um, have no panties on and I'm wearing a dress." I said not wanting to look Tate in the eye.

His lips drew in a thin line as he had a pained look on his face.

"Tate, nothing happened. Sam tried...but...John barged in and..."

"Thank God. I'm still going to kill them, but I'm glad to know it…in that case, I'll never tell what I saw when I found you, that is my little secret…my bright spot in a sea of darkness. But Reese, I almost got sick when I saw the bruises all over you." I thought, how could any guy physically be this handsome, and at least at this moment, so compassionate?

He looked away from me, utterly disgusted at what that freak had done to me. I was a little more worried now, I hadn't seen the bruises yet, but I could sure feel them. I was sore all over.

I walked in the bathroom and he followed me.

"Um Tate, I can handle this…I looked from him to the toilet and back." Blushing I said, "I'll call you when I need you."

Just knowing he was outside the door I could barely stand to use the bathroom. I was trying to process all that had happened. When I was done I looked at myself in the mirror. Oh my, I wish I hadn't. I looked horrible, my mascara was smeared, my hair an unruly mess, and my dress all wrinkled. Not to mention the most obvious, I had a horrific black eye. I scared myself just looking at me.

I tried to wipe my mascara under my eyes away, and tame my hair a little before I opened the door.

"Tate, I had no idea I looked this bad."

"I try not to think about how you look Reese. I want to kill that son of a bitch." He truly was seething. I was a little worried about what he might eventually do.

"We are not together any more Tate, this is not your problem, please don't get involved."

"Are you kidding me, I don't care if you hate me." I raised an eyebrow at his comment. "I will kill anyone who hurts you Reese." He slowly stopped in the hallway and turned to me.

"Like me or not, I can't let someone hurt you. I…God Reese, I care about you so much…" He looked like he wanted to say something else but stopped.

Tears almost sprang to my eyes. "Tate, I'm going to lie down in my bed for a little while. I may not see…"

He quickly cut me off "Oh I'm not going anywhere, you can bet on that."

"Suit yourself."

I literally didn't think I could stand up any more. I was fighting a losing battle to exhaustion. Tate walked me to my bed and stood there until I was lying down, then he covered me up.

# CHAPTER 18

'm not sure how long I slept, but I woke up to sunshine pouring through my window. My eyes were fuzzy, especially my black eye. I started to sit up, but I ached all over. I let out a long sigh, and turned to my side. That's when I almost jumped out of my bed, regardless of the pain.

Tate was lying on his side staring at me, silently.

"Tate, what are you doing in here, you shouldn't be in my room," I said breathlessly.

"I'm sorry Reese, but I couldn't stand it. I've been dying to get you alone to talk about what happened between us for two weeks. Hurt or not, I need some questions answered." His voice was even and calm, and mesmerizing actually. I had missed this voice so much.

"I really have nothing to say to you Tate. You're wasting your time."

"Ok then, can I ask you a few questions, I'll keep 'em simple?"

I didn't speak, I just laid on my back and stared at the ceiling.

"Ok first, did you enjoy our kiss at the hospital, the night before you….dumped me?"

"I, Uh,"

"Just answer the question please."

There was a long pause..."Yes" I inwardly cringed, admitting it after all he had done.

I could hear the happy tone in his smile...uhhh. I could tell this wasn't going to go well.

"Ok second, did you enjoy spending time with me, and having me as your boyfriend for the last...well, nearly a year?"

"That's two questions Tate."

"Please just answer them."

"Yes and yes"

By the look on his face, he seemed shocked and confused. So I quickly followed.

"That was before I learned what you were really like Tate."

"What do you ...I mean okay, now we're getting somewhere, you're finally talking with me." He said very calmly. "I'm guessing you came to this...conclusion about me the night you quit calling or answering my calls. I'm also guessing it had to come from Carter, since right after you met with him, you broke up with me."

I was silent for a few moments.

"Reese?" He turned my chin tenderly to look at him.

"Please, I've been dying over here...I need to know what you think I did...please!" he begged.

"Really Tate, you have not been dying. You quickly got over me...us. I heard all about the pictures on Facebook from the beach this last couple of days."

"What...who...I mean, Facebook? What kind of pictures?"

"Carter, I mean my mom said it was obvious you were having a blast. I heard about the photos with girls who were half dressed and drinking."

"Wait, you first said Carter. He told you this? And... you've been talking with him, but not me...He left you, and basically dropped off the face of the earth. I had to pick up his leftovers Reese, which I gladly did, and you're talking to him and not me."

*Pick up the leftovers?*

"Tate, I haven't actually talked with him, he texted me. And you're right. It seems every guy in my life has turned out to be nothing like I hoped."

I stared right at him, knowing I had just hurt him. His expression was pained.

"First of all Reese, I was miserable at the beach. Finn and I both were actually. We had some girls that tried really hard, ridiculously so, to get us out of our funk, but we didn't give in. Most of the snapshots that were taken, the girls staged, by all crowding around us as we sat by the pool. Most of them, we didn't smile in, but one or two we did, because someone was doing something stupid like funnel a beer right in front of us, or fake passing out...you know."

He touched my hand and I drew it back quickly. "I love you Reese," he said. My eyes went wide. "How could you doubt that?"

So it was true. He finally admitted it.

"You may think you love me Tate, but you couldn't possibly respect me. I know about...Lisa...I know how you broke up their marriage."

He looked stunned and ...upset, "Wait, I...did Carter tell you that too?"

I shrugged my shoulders, and said "I should have figured it out on my own anyhow. I noticed strange behavior at the

125

hospital between you and her. I wondered how she even knew you that well. She's my mom's good friend, and I had never heard mention of you from her."

"Also, she was in an awful mood when she found us… uh…kissing," I said. I blushed when I talked about our last kiss.

"And third, Carter walked in on Lisa and Tony arguing about you the night he wrecked his car. That was the first time he knew you were the reason his parents had separated. He also blames our break up on you too."

Tate sighed and ran his hand through his hair.

"I didn't know if Carter knew," he said as he stared at the wall.

"That's all you have to say? I give you this chance to talk with me and…well…at least you didn't deny it." I tried to get up off the bed. He gently held me down.

"Reese, I need you to know what really happened…please, just listen to me, then ask questions." He said as he looked at me through the corner of his eyes…as if truly, embarrassment was consuming him.

I motioned my hand in the air as if to say, by all means Tate, go ahead.

And so he began…

"I was helping out with the hardware store on Main Street in the afternoons. My dad had set it up, so I could 'gain responsibility' once I had gotten my license. He wanted me to learn how to manage the money I made weekly. One day, I was downstairs loading sheetrock onto the back of this guy's truck when I heard yelling. It sounded as if it were a man and woman, so I got really nervous, not sure of what was happening. I ran around the corner to find Tony and Lisa Davis in a heated argument. I recognized them from school events, and realized they were Carter's parents.

"I pretended to go to the lumber scrap piles near where they were, worried I would have to call the cops or something. That's how loud they were. As I got closer to them, I heard him calling her filthy names for forgetting to leave him his dry cleaning out before his trip. She was in tears and told him she didn't realize she was supposed to. He backhanded her then, hard and she fell into the side of the car. I couldn't help but catch a glimpse of her face...she was...she was terrified. I was the only one to witness this...crazy shit.

"I stood there, dumbfounded for a while, not sure what to do. Then I heard her apologize, even though she was the one slapped, by a man no doubt. He got in her face and shoved her again making her head go back. He was muttering 'you aren't good for anything are you?'

"He went back inside to pay for some cinder block, and I saw it as my chance to see if she was alright. She was sobbing hysterically when I went up to her. At first she was embarrassed and tried to hide her face. Then as I put my hand on her shoulder to see if I could help her, she just fell into my arms. I didn't know what to do, so I took her to the other side of the car. Knowing if Tony walked out and saw her leaning on me, he would kill her, and maybe even me. So I was trying to conceal her. She relaxed a little, just being held. She thanked me immensely, and then asked for my number so she could buy me lunch sometime. I really just think she wanted someone to talk to that wouldn't beat her up, you know.

"I was scared, angry, and excited that this gorgeous, 'older' woman was going to buy me lunch. I knew it was wrong, but she was so weak, so frail, and blatantly abused that I convinced myself it would be okay. But, I also figured it would never happen.

"Well, I couldn't have been more wrong. She called me the next day, a Saturday, and asked to meet at the Cafe West. I went, expecting to get a free meal and a few thank yous but I also expected her to ask for me to keep her fight with Tony private.

"I actually got part of that right. She did thank me over and over and then she cried a little too. She shared with me things that were happening in her life, things that shocked and appalled me. I had no idea Carter's parents had so many issues. The crazy part, was she was taking up for Tony in a way. She said he was struggling at work and so his anger always got the best of him at home.

"But, then she started coming down to the store to see me, pretending to pick up caulk or hangers. She would linger downstairs with me. Finally, one evening before closing, she asked if we could take a ride. We went down to the lake and sat on the beach and talked for hours. She told me about the years of abuse that she had taken from Tony, mostly emotional, and how she was stuck in her marriage. It was cold, so we scooted closer together and I let her borrow my jacket. She reached over and grabbed my hand and leaned her head on my shoulder. I should have known then what her intentions were. I mean, she was an incredibly wounded woman who was receiving comfort she hadn't had from a guy in years.

"The last time I was with her alone, was when Lisa had asked for me to deliver some patio rocks to her house. I brought them during the afternoon, Tony happened to be at work. It was a 90 degree day and humid, and I was there for about an hour. She had leaned out the door and asked me to come in for lemonade. I had my shirt pulled up my chest and folded under, trying to cool off a little. So ice cold lemonade and air conditioning, seemed like a great idea.

"I was standing beside her table, drinking the cool beverage when she walked over to me, and hugged me. I felt a little awkward but I said, 'thank you' and hugged her back. I just assumed she needed a friend like before. Then she started rubbing my back and she reached up and started kissing me. I was totally taken aback. I mean Lisa is a beautiful woman and all, but she is married and much older than me. She kept kissing me and wouldn't back off, even when I turned my face. She used her hand and turned my head back to her. Her kiss deepened. Then she jerked my shirt over my head. She reached for my jeans, and started to unbutton them.

"I should have not even gone in. And I certainly should have walked away when she started groping me. But I was shocked. And frankly, I was a little turned on that she would want me like this. I kept seeing her face as it looked when Tony had hit her that day, and I felt I was sort of helping her.

"She took off her top and kept kissing me. Then she undid her bra and took my hand to feel of her breast. I couldn't believe it was happening. Here we were, nearly naked standing in front of each other when the unthinkable happened...Tony walked in.

"I guess with the music she was playing in the kitchen, and our breathing being so loud, we didn't hear him. He froze in the doorway, and then when he registered what was happening, he ran to me, knocking me on the floor. Then he literally smacked Lisa so hard she nearly flew across the room. I quickly jumped to my feet, and rammed my body into his. He was yelling obscene words my direction. We jumped up ready to go at it again, when he looked at Lisa, spit in her direction, and said I could have her, she wasn't worth it.

"That was the last time we were alone. Nothing more physical ever happened. Tony left town as did Carter, once his father told him what a 'cheating whore' his mom was. He seemed to think we had sex. Lisa said he wouldn't believe her when she told him over and over that we hadn't. The sad part is when I think about the moment in her kitchen, I'm scared to think about what might have happened, if he hadn't walked in.

"I did call to check on her for a couple of weeks. At first she was withdrawn and depressed. Then she seemed to realize that at least she wasn't being beat up anymore. So she would text me frequently, and suggest we meet. I knew it was wrong, and not wanting to hurt her anymore than she had already been, I would always have excuses. You and I had started talking then too, and I would in no way have jeopardized losing the chance to get closer to you. She knew I was seeing someone, she just didn't have any idea it was you. I can imagine though, once we got closer, your mom must have told her. Lisa would send me updates on how she hoped you and Carter would get back together when he came back home. That's when I realized she was still hung up on me. I got to the point where I wouldn't even respond to her texts. I was furious that she thought you would get back with Carter. In fact, I wouldn't put it past her to have agreed to get back with Tony just to bring Carter back to town. She wanted the two of you together, and the two of us apart that much.

"So the first time we had seen each other since the event nearly a year before, was at the hospital when I came to find you. In the hallway, when you saw us, she asked me if we, meaning her and me, could go back to the way we were. Especially, since you and Carter were back together. She said she missed me. I told her no, of course. She acted fine, but I knew she was upset." Tate let out a long sigh.

〰️

I was dazed by all of the confessions Tate had just given. In some ways, I completely understood. He was young and she was beautiful. He was always one to try and help out. I guess he realized he wasn't willing to help out that much in the end. I was even more shocked that Lisa was trying to orchestrate my getting back with Carter, for her own benefit, and making Tate think that I would.

"Reese, please say something. I had no idea Lisa was what was in your head all of this time. I thought it truly was Carter. I have been dying. I…I was…I *am* in love with you and your leaving has nearly killed me.

I looked over to Tate with a newfound awe. I wasn't sure what I was feeling, but I knew it was no longer hatred.

I scooted over a little closer, and reached up to rub his face. He closed his eyes and let out a low sigh.

"Tate, I'm so sorry. You really didn't sleep with Lisa?"

"No, no way"

"And you haven't been with her, not once since we started dating last year?"

His face came closer to mine and he whispered… "no way Reese."

"Oh God, I'm so sorry I doubted you. Carter told me his dad said you slept with her. I wonder if Lisa told you the truth. Who knows, she may have really told Tony y'all did sleep together. It sounds like she had developed strong feelings for you."

"I'm not sure what she told him. Knowing how much she wanted to take a little back of what he had taken from her over the years, she may have lied. But Reese, that is not who I am. Even if he hadn't walked in, I don't believe when it came down to it, I would have let it get that far. I know I wouldn't have. She had a family. Did she need to get away from him then, yes, but I knew better than to let it be with me."

My eyes were fixed on his. "I'm just sorry we wasted all this time. I mean if we had been together, I could have avoided last night and nearly getting raped again."

Squeezing my eyes tightly shut, I quickly realized what I had just said. I tried to move on to another topic but Tate caught on fast.

"What did you just say? You were almost raped 'again?'… what does that mean?" With fear in his eyes he leaned back to see my face better.

"I…um…Oh God Tate. I can't tell you. I just can't."

"The hell you can't Reese, I have to know, what are you talking about? Who did something to you?" His face was suddenly red and his eyes scorching.

I let out a long sigh, and rolled on to my back so I wouldn't have to face him. As I started talking, I threw my arm up over my face to hide the pain and embarrassment in my eyes.

"It's a long story Tate, I really would rather you not know okay?"

Tate's eyes were glazing over, like maybe he was fearful of what I was going to say or anger for who did it. I'm not sure, but I became emotional all of a sudden. I put both hands to my face and my shoulders started to shake. After the last few hours, and facing Tate with his truth and now mine, it was more than I could take.

"Hey, Reese, I'm here. Please don't cry. He reached for my face, tenderly lifting my chin up so I would look at him. "Can I hold you?"

I shook my head yes, desperately wanting to be held. His arms felt like home. I had missed them so much. I saw a trust and deep love in his gorgeous hazel, brown eyes. When I laid my head on his chest, I could hear his heart racing just like mine.

"Oh God Reese, I'm sorry for all you've been through. How do you manage to be as good as you are, with your history not holding you back, huh?"

I took several minutes to gain my composure before I could talk.

"Tate, I'm afraid to tell you. No one but basically my parents and Elle know about this. I still can hardly stand to talk about it. But mostly, I'm afraid you'll look at me differently. I won't be the pure, wholesome girl you fell for last year, you know?"

"Oh Reese you crazy girl, there is nothing that you could ever tell me that could make me think less of you...I...Uhhhh," he let out a long sigh, "how can you not know how much I adore you?"

His words made my heart flutter "Okay, but promise me... promise me this will be the last time we ever talk about it."

"Reese, I don't know if I can promise that." I stared at him and gave out a big breath. "Okay, I promise...now tell me," he said through his teeth. This time I could tell it was anger emanating off of him, but not for me.

I tilted my chin down a little just remembering how awful I must look from my attack last night. "Okay, well...about a little over a year ago I was at Elle's party with the girls and Carter. She was having a house party and then I was going to stay the night with her. About 9:30 or so, at least that's what they tell me, I started feeling bad, like dizzy and sick on my stomach. I just wanted to lie down, but I felt so strange that I decided just to go home. Elle tried to convince me to stay, or for her to take me. But it was her party and she couldn't leave. Carter couldn't take me either. He had told his mom he would pick something up for her and I knew he would be heading the opposite direction from my house. He said he thought I would be staying with Elle, so he had planned to do this for his mom. So I drove myself. By the time I sat in my car, my vision was a little blurry. It took me a while to even pull out of her driveway. I don't remember a lot after that. I vaguely remember someone touching me, and talking to me, but I don't remember anything else. That is, until I woke up. When I leaned up to look at the time in my car and try to figure out where I was, I screamed." I quickly turned away from Tate, "I'm sorry, I can't tell you anymore."

"Please Reese, I have to know. I'm here, I'm not going anywhere, now please finish." His arms tightened around me. I couldn't stand torturing him like this, or me for that matter.

I found the courage to continue. "I hurt and felt strange. When I looked down, my dress and panties had...they had blood on them Tate, I had been raped. Date raped they said. I lost my virginity without wanting to." I was sobbing by this point, "I don't even know who did this to me...I...I was so scared." My tears were rolling, Tate's eyes were red too, he couldn't catch my tears fast enough with his thumbs.

"I didn't want anyone to know, I...wasn't sure if I had led someone on, I was pretty sure I hadn't, but I couldn't help wondering. Of course, there was a police report. My parents were so upset and wanted to find who did this to me. I just wanted it to be over. They did tests," I looked at Tate and cringed, "you know, to make sure I wasn't pregnant or hadn't contracted any diseases. But they also took DNA in case they could match it. I called Elle. She was so wonderful to stay with me for a while. I was devastated though. Carter, well he was gone. I had gotten one last text from him saying he couldn't bear to tell me goodbye, but then I rarely heard from him. Knowing I might never see him again, I was afraid to let him know what had happened to me, afraid he would think badly of me. He hurt me too for just leaving and not looking back. For so long, even after I met you, I questioned everyone and everything. Just when I was beginning to feel better about myself and really fall for you, I learned what you had done. In my head, I had been let down by guys. First there was my rapist, then Carter, then you, now John and my attacker."

I turned to look at Tate, dreading to look in his face. "What is wrong with me Tate, why is it okay to hurt me?"

What I saw in his eyes was remorse…Love…pain.

"Reese," he drug my name out slowly. "I couldn't love you anymore than I love you right now. Please, let me protect you. I…I'm sorry you thought that I had hurt you. That would *never* happen. And if I can help it, no one will *ever* hurt you again." He hugged me, trying not to squeeze too hard because of all of my bruises.

"Will you let me? Will you let me take care of you?" he said.

"Oh Tate," I was crying even harder.

# CHAPTER 19

ate reached over and pulled the blanket over us, up to our chins. Then he put his arms around me, stroking my back. Leaning in, he gave me a soft kiss on the lips. Still close to my face, and exhaling slowly he said "I want you to never worry about a guy hurting you again, okay. I want to be here for you always. Then he started trailing his lips down my neck and over my collarbone." The feeling was...amazing. I couldn't believe after last night I could allow myself to relax to a guy's touch. But his was, soothing and healing.

When his lips found mine again, I didn't hold back. I kissed him, leaving no room for interpretation. His tongue touched mine, sending shivers down my back and legs. Then our kiss deepened further, and his hands slid down to my waist and then my backside. The pain from the bruise on my hip startled me, causing me to stop. I grabbed the covers tight with my hands, and pulled them up to my chin gasping.

"Oh my, I don't have on any panties Tate, remember?"

A soft grin came across his lips. "I'll stop then if you want me to Reese. I'll never push you to do anything you don't want to do. I've just missed you so much, and seeing you like this...

I need to know you want me to be near you, holding you, understanding you in every way."

"I love that you are. I will never doubt you again. I just don't want to sleep with you Tate. I'm just not ready yet. I vowed to my parents and myself I would wait until my wedding night." I said as I dropped my gaze down to the bed, away from his eyes.

"Hey, I don't think you're ready yet either. Let's take it slow. I love you Reese. I plan to stay here this week if that's okay. I have already talked to Elle about it, Finn is staying too. We want to be here for you guys."

The thought of me having even longer with Tate was an amazing, settling feeling. I was so glad he was here. "I think that's a wonderful idea Tate. I...I can't believe we get to spend a whole week together." I felt foolish grinning like a school girl, but I was suddenly happy as a lark.

Tate on the other hand went quickly from happy to concerned looking. "Can I ask you something Reese?" I nodded yes, "Did you like him, John, did you like him? Elle said how handsome he was and how rich he was. Was he nice to you? Did you have...a good time with him otherwise?"

"Do you mean did I kiss him? Is that what you really want to know?"

He looked at me with a glare of trepidation over my impending answer. "I did Tate." I let out a long exhale, "I'm sorry, I had too much to drink and was overly relaxed. Something I swore I wouldn't do, but I was so upset over the Facebook pictures that I thought I was kind of getting you back, you know. Me hanging out with another guy I felt in some way would hurt you back. I wasn't thinking. I really was wrong about him I guess. I truly thought though...I mean he seemed so genuine. His friends," I said with disgust "not so much."

"I can't believe I was ultimately the reason you ran in to another guys arms Reese. I can't believe that guy let you get attacked." His words came out a hiss.

"He was up on the top deck trying to get me a snack, so I wouldn't feel bad later for having drinks on an empty stomach. I went down to use the rest room and look for Chloe. I guess there was too much space and time between us for him to keep Sam from attacking me." I got a chill from head to toe thinking about Sam's eyes as they pierced into me and his mouth all over me.

"I think before I lay here with you any longer, I need to wash Sam off of me. I can't help but remember all he did... thank God I remember what he *didn't* get a chance to do."

"Let me help you in the bathtub okay?" He winked at me. "You're too weak to stand in the shower," he said as he reached over and pulled the covers off of me, helping me to stand.

"I think you're probably right."

"You're not going to protest...you know, about me seeing you...naked?"

I looked at him with a sheepish grin, "No, I guess I'm not..."

"Oh shit Reese, I...where did this confidence come from?"

"Thanks, I think...but I'm sure when you see the bruises I won't be so 'hot' then."

He grinned as he walked me down the hall. Everyone was standing in the living room and they started coming towards me, as I was nearing the bathroom.

"How are you feeling?" Elle asked softly as she rubbed my shoulder.

"I rested some, now I just want to wash the filth off of me… you know, of Sam," I said.

Good idea. And Reese, we tracked down your phone. Looks like there is only one cab company for Beaufort, like Maura said. Finn is meeting the cab driver in Morehead City to claim it."

"Oh good, tell Finn thanks for me. I'm glad I'll still have it. I need to call my mom later today.

⁓

Tate filled the tub up with water while I sat on the seat by the vanity. I still had my dress on, eagerly awaiting him to pour in bubbles…oh good, bubbles were better to hide me with. I still couldn't believe he was here, and that we were making up. His story over Lisa was awful. I had no idea what her and Tony's marriage had actually been like, or that she still wanted Tate.

The worst part about our talk earlier was that Tate KNEW now. There was no going back. He knew I was no longer a virgin, and he knew I didn't know who had done it. I was worried now that it would drive him crazy. I tried to think of how I would feel if I were him, and I know I would be dying to find the person responsible.

I wanted Tate and me to move forward and put the past completely behind us. Was that possible? Once all of the reality sunk in for him, would he still be there for me? I was also worried that after all that I had been through, I would rely on him too much. I didn't want to suffocate him, and I didn't want to lose myself by needing him. I resolved to take it one day at a time. I looked over at Tate, for now I had this glorious guy in my life. I didn't intend on letting him go.

"Reese, are you okay? Are you ready to get in?" Tate softly touched my arm.

"Um, yeah, thank you Tate. I really am okay. Why don't you go see if Finn is back?" Now, I wasn't sure about him seeing me undress. We had NEVER been that open and intimate before.

"I want to help you. I...I'm afraid you aren't steady enough yet. How about if you hold onto the sink, I'll close my eyes and pull your dress over your head, okay? We already know that is all you have on to remove," he said with a raise of his eyebrow.

I was worried he was still picturing Sam tearing my panties off. I know I still was. I didn't want him to think I didn't appreciate all he was doing for me. "Okay, as long as you keep your eyes closed." I eyed him suspiciously. "I know I have to look hideous right now."

"Never Reese. I...I still can't think about what could have happened to you. God, what has happened to you...I'm still trying to wrap my head around it."

"Tate, please don't...don't look at me differently. I'm okay. Really, I just have a lot to work through. Believe it or not, I've done well so far. But, I can't stand to think of you looking at me differently. I'm still the same Reese you said you fell in love with."

Tate was silent for a brief period, just staring at me. I had no idea what he was thinking. "Will you please get into this bath I just fixed for you? The water will get cold if you don't get in soon. Here, let me help you."

I was shy to let him take off my dress. But as he gripped the bottom hem, I was feeling more and more weak...from the last 24 hours, to seeing him here in front of me. I wasn't sure, but one thing I was sure of, I was in love with this man.

As I stood there naked before him, quickly taking the step into the tub, I heard him inhale sharply. "Reese...I...Oh God, I want to always be here for you. Please let me. Let me protect you from all of this madness. Life can be so hard...but for you Reese, I can't bear it to be that way. I...love you.

I was sitting in the bubbles feeling like I was wrapped in his warmth. He had knelt down beside of me and was looking into my eyes. I almost lost it staring back at him.

"Tate, how can you still be here? I told you what happened to me early last year, and you know I was attacked, almost raped last night. How...Why do you want to stay? Don't you see, I'm a walking disaster? Trouble finds me. It doesn't want to let me go. I'm...I'm used Tate..." I was sobbing again. What the hell was wrong with me?

He grabbed my face with both hands and made me look at him...my shoulders shaking. "You...You didn't ask for any of this Reese. You were a victim. Don't you understand? It doesn't make me want to run, it makes me want you more... want to protect you...to save you, to love you...more." he reached down and gently touched my lips with his. "Please don't take that from me...I need you, I want you...just like you are."

What is he thinking? He should find someone with less problems. I will only bring him down. Ugh! How can he be so good to me? "Tate..."

"We better stop now before I decide to climb in there with you...I would...I'd get soaking wet if it meant I could be that close to you."

I laughed out loud at the image of him soaking wet...then, I'm not sure what got into me, I reached for his hand and held my lips up to his, like I was going to kiss him. But as he started to stand up, I pulled him in, clothes and all. We both screamed, and I laughed out loud. He did too...at least until he realized he was in the tub with me and I was naked. His face turned red and he looked at me like 'you did it'. I suddenly was regretting my brash decision. He immediately pulled me on top of him, so I was straddling his lap. My breasts exposed. He leaned up and kissed me slowly at first, then more intense, his lips softly moving with mine. He inhaled deeply as did I. I had chill bumps down my body while he kissed me. I was the first one to move away from his lips, this time to move onto his neck. He let out a deep groan, as I moved my lips back to his ear and breathing in his ear, I heard his breath catch. I felt his arousal underneath me. I was instantly frozen. As soon as I realized what was happening, I quickly sat back to the other side of the tub.

"Reese, don't stop." But as he realized I was sitting alone, his equilibrium became balanced, and he looked nervous. He quickly sat up, looking at me to make sure we were still okay. He started to get up, then he lightly grabbed my arm. "I'm so sorry. I didn't mean to get that out of control. I...I can't hardly control myself around you Reese. I want you so bad. But, I respect that you don't want me that way....yet. I'm sorry."

He looked lost, mortified. It was as much my fault as it was his. I had to tell him how much I wanted him too. He was so distracting. I was looking at how his shirt stuck to his wet body pronouncing his muscles, and how his hair was curling up a little from the steam of the tub. His beautiful brown, hazel eyes were pleading with me to be okay.

"Tate, it was my fault. I got carried away. I...I'm just so glad to have you here with me. So glad to know the truth about," I looked shyly at him, "about you and Lisa. I'm just glad you want to be here...if you really do."

He shifted a little and stared into my eyes. "I don't want to be anywhere else," he said. With that he grabbed a towel from the stack and rose out of the tub. I couldn't help but feel a pain of disappointment from the separation. But, I knew it was for the best. I couldn't lose my self-control. It was really all I had left.

"Tate, I'm sorry for," I motioned to the tub "you know." I hadn't meant to get him so worked up and then stop.

"Oh Reese, I'm sorry. I get so carried away when I'm with you. I want you so badly...it's hard for me to think straight. Much less when I get to feel so much of you." He looked at me then quickly back to the door turning his back on me. "How about call me when you're done. I'll be waiting right outside the door." He looked at me once more, then with a long sigh he walked out of the bathroom.

I had to admit it felt so good to be that close with him. But I don't know how long I can resist him. I felt I better keep my distance. There is certainly no lack of desire between us.

I washed up, still thoroughly disgusted with my bruises. For a moment John flashed into my mind. I didn't know what he might be thinking, or what happened with him. On one hand I was SO thankful that he barged in and attacked Sam when he did. But on the other hand, he was responsible for inviting me into that situation. Ugh...why didn't I have a better judge of people, mainly guys? I was really disturbed at how wrong I had read him. My heart had told me he was such a great guy. My brain, on the other hand, must have taken a temporary vacation.

I carefully got up and dried off, wrapping my hair in a towel and putting my bathrobe on. I took a minute to take my eye make-up off and reapply some mascara with a little blush, and light lip gloss. I was putting on lotion when the door cracked open followed by a soft knock.

"Reese," Tate whispered. "You okay?" he looked disappointed. "I thought I was going to help you get out and get dressed. Are you not quite as weak now?"

I chuckled out loud. "I think I'm feeling better...are you sure that was the only reason you wanted to help me?"

"Come here you." He wrapped me in his arms. "I'm so glad you're okay." He put his chin on my forehead, and let out a content breath. "Hey, why don't you get your coffee from the kitchen, and rest on the couch. Elle put you in one of your favorite movies, *Dirty Dancing*," he raised his eyebrows up and down real quick. I laughed, but inside I was thinking back to the dirty dancing I did with John last night. Well, okay, not really dirty, but sensual. Oh Tate, I thought, I'm so sorry I didn't believe in you more.

"That sounds wonderful. Let me plug in my phone first so it can be charging. I need to call my mom too." I reached up and swiftly touched my lips to Tate's then walked into my room.

"Okay. And Finn and I are going to run to the store. I'll call you before we head back to see if there's anything you need." He called after me.

"Thanks!" I said. I was dying to plug in my phone and see what messages I had.

# CHAPTER 20

decided to get dressed too so I threw on a soft cotton sundress, panties of course, and braided my damp hair to the side. There, now I felt normal again...almost. After my phone had enough charge to turn it on, I quickly started going through my messages. I was sickened again, as I started reading Elle's and Maura's frantic texts. They were so scared for me. Oh girls, I was so worried for you too, I thought. Then I stopped on one from John from 4am.

I can't begin to tell you how sorry

I am Reese. Elle told me Tate is on his way. Please, let him take care of you.

You're going to need him. I sent that SOB Sam back home after nearly killing him. Please forgive me for allowing that to happen to you.

I blame myself.

Love, J

Then another at 9 am (It was now noon).

> Don't be mad at Elle, but she tells me you're okay.
>
> Tate did rescue you. I will be forever grateful. I keep thanking God Sam didn't succeed. I know it's soon, but I need to see you.
>
> Please let me Reese - Love J

What in the world, "Elle!" I started hollering. I walked quickly through the house to find my dear, back-stabbing FRIEND! I cannot believe her.

"Reese are you okay? What's wrong? Oh good you're dressed and..."

I quickly cut her off. "Don't you dare 'oh good' me Elle. Why have you been texting John information about me? I can't believe after all that happened you would do that."

Looking like a deer in headlights, she finally let her shoulders relax. "Reese, I'm sorry, but you have no idea how he reacted last night. I couldn't say it in front of Tate, but that guy was absolutely distraught. I was afraid he would jump overboard with guilt. He was crying, and begging me to find someone to help you. *He* suggested I call Tate."

The realization was mystifying. I couldn't believe he would do that. "What happened after I left Elle?" I looked to her, slowly sitting down on the couch.

"John just lost it Reese. That guy has got it so bad for you. I think in one day he was falling for you. I know you don't want to hear that, but he was. And, I think he is genuinely a good guy, who just has shit for friends. He literally knocked Sam out cold. But like I said, not before Sam got in a few hard hits. He bruised John badly and cracked a couple of his ribs, I think. Afterwards, he and Harrison, who also seems like one of the good guys, helped him tie Sam up."

I was staring at her in disbelief.

"I know, crazy right. But, he did. He tied him to the end of the bed in the room you two were in."

I cringed just thinking about being in there with Sam.

"Then he came out yelling for you, assuming you were still there. That's when he lost it Reese. He was pacing the floor and running his hands through his hair like he was going to explode, or breakdown. We weren't sure which one or when. I told him what you had done by taking a cab. He called you every minute like a crazy man. When he found out Tate was on his way to find you, he physically relaxed a little. He grilled me about Tate though. He seemed to want confirmation that he was making the right choice by having me call him."

I was shaking my head...totally amazed.

"Then I heard him on the phone to his Dad and Sam's Dad. He basically told them everything. Sam's Dad sent a car after him and as far as I know, he was heading back down to Charlotte by 9am this morning. Brett was another story. Chloe passed out and finally quit throwing up. And then once we knew you were safe, John and Harrison offered to carry Chloe to your jeep, so we could get to you quicker. Chloe had started sobering up then, and Brett woke up. I cussed him out Reese. I mean hardcore, and I don't do that. He seemed sorry, but John said he had done drugs in college at least once, and must have gotten these from Sam. John claimed to not know he had any last night.

That brings us to John's texts to me. He was worried Reese. I saw how upset he was, so I thought I should relieve his pain a little bit, and update him. Please don't be mad." She looked at me with tired eyes.

"Well, when you put it like that, I guess it's hard to be mad at you." I grabbed Elle's hand, and she hugged me. Ugh John! Why did you have to choose such screwed up friends? I mean you did seem like a great guy, I thought to myself. "But, I've got Tate anyway." I gave a sideways glance to Elle.

"Oh thank God. He has been another tortured soul texting me the last few days for updates. You know he thought you were back with Carter." She said with a guilty little look.

"I know, he told me," I said. "Do you happen to know anything about that?" I eyed her suspiciously. She gave a shrug of her shoulders. But I knew.

"So, what about Lisa? Isn't that still a mess?"

Elle asked, quickly changing the subject.

I explained the whole Lisa situation. When I finished, Elle was shocked and sad for everyone involved from Carter to Lisa but especially for Tate. After all, he had been suffering for over two weeks, being away from me and not knowing why.

"Well, I guess you have a whole new meaning of the need for communication, don't you? If only you would have talked to Tate," she said. I had been thinking the same thing. I was truly frustrated how I had handled things.

Maura, Chloe, and Elle were all out on the beach. I had decided since the guys were gone for a little while, I would go for a walk, to try to clear my head. I walked towards the point at the end of the beach, the opposite way of where we laid out. It was a serene place. A spot where the beach was so wide it looked like a desert. It was called The Point because the beach literally makes a point and the waters meet and form a crash, or explosion together; instead of the usual rolling of waves in to the shore. It was peaceful, and it almost felt like your troubles could be smashed away here...and drift out to sea. I was thinking and silently praying, when I noticed someone walking towards me. Immediately I knew... it was John. Oh God, how did he find me? As he got closer, he spoke loudly...

"Reese, I promise I'm not stalking you. I know I've said that before, but it's true." As he got closer, his voice got softer. "I was coming to see you one way or another. I was walking up the beach, hoping to find a way to convince you, when I saw Elle. She didn't see me. You weren't with them, so I waited to see if you would come out. Then you did, but you walked in the opposite direction. I saw you were alone, and figured it would be my best shot. I hope you aren't afraid...of me." He reached out to touch my face and I stepped back. "My God Reese, your eye..." He looked down at his feet, an emotion I wasn't sure how to describe crossed the features of his face. "I should have never let this happen to you." He looked back up at me, this time his eyes were pleading forgiveness. "Will you ever forgive me Reese? What if he hadn't stopped? What if I hadn't gotten down there in time? Ahhh," he growled "I could kill him."

I had to stop this torture he was causing himself. I reached out and touched his hand. "Stop John. I've already forgiven you. Elle told me all about how you acted after I left. I know you didn't mean for it to happen. I also know you told her to call Tate." He quickly looked off to the side, shaking his head like he was still questioning that decision. "I think you're a good man John. Like Elle says, you just have shit for friends. I'll be okay. But you, you need to find new, friends." I let out a sad laugh.

He reached up and touched his fingers to my cheek. I didn't step back, but I did turn away a little. "So, are you back with Tate now? Is he still here?"

"Yes and Yes." I whispered the words. I hated to hurt him more, and I knew he would blame himself again.

"Even though you were sure you wanted him out of your life before?" Those words he nearly cried.

"I never wanted him out of my life John, I thought he had done something...something that would have made it necessary for us to be apart. But it turns out, he didn't. In fact, we've discovered we should have never even been apart. And we..." He turned to face the ocean. "John, I'm sorry about the kiss... or kisses," I blushed.

He turned to face me and reached out to hold onto both of my arms. "Well I'm not sorry Reese. I never will be. I was wrong to have Elle call Tate for you. Please, just think about it." He reached up, touching my face again. "I'll be here for ten more days before my boat leaves. You have my number, text me...please."

Before I could answer either way, I saw a figure of someone coming near us, then I heard "Reese?" I turned around and Tate was searching my eyes, concerned for who this was with me. I wasn't sure what to do.

"Um, Tate, this is...John. He was just checking to make sure I was okay."

"John, as in Sam's John? What the hell are you doing here?" He got close to John's face - these two beautiful men side by side - then he said "It would be best if you NEVER speak to Reese again, you got that?" as he jabbed his finger in John's chest."

My breath caught, why would he have to do that? John just looked at me. I could tell he wanted to talk to me longer. But, evidently feeling the guilt he still had, he implored forgiveness one more time with his eyes. Then he held his hands up, and turned around...walking away.

Tate turned to me and pausing for a second, he said, "Why were you here with him? I saw..." He looked confused... "I saw him touching your face Reese. Please tell me you don't want to see him again. I don't know if I can stand this. He was responsible for putting you in danger. You know that right? He is no good. Okay?"

I looked at Tate. I wanted to tell him that I didn't blame John. That John was good after all, but my brain wouldn't let me. "It's okay Tate," I walked into his arms, loving his embrace. "I'm yours, you know that. There's nothing to be worried about."

He hugged me tight, exhaling hard. Then he looked down and said, "hey, let's go back to the house. We can relax on the beach and forget about him and last night. I came to find you, because I called and you didn't answer." He reached down and gave me a kiss. "I got worried about you."

We walked hand in hand to the house. The breeze felt amazing. But if I'm honest, I have to admit I was a little saddened by how John and I had left it. I know Tate and I are together. I love him, no doubt. But, I do hate how he treated John. I guess if the roles had been reversed I would have been upset too.

We laid out on the beach for hours. The sun felt amazing, as did the easy music, and the presence of Tate right beside of me. I couldn't believe how much things had changed. But, it seemed all was right with the world again.

# CHAPTER 21

Elle and Finn came running up to us with keys in their hands. They were grinning from ear to ear. "Okay guys, time to be on the water," said Finn. I thought what in the world is he talking about? "Do you mean in the water?" I asked him, with a confused look on my face.

Tate shot to his feet "Oh yeah! Let's do this," he said. Then he paused holding out his hand, "That is if you feel up to it Reese?"

I was lost. What were they talking about? Tate pulled me up and started ushering me towards the end of the point again. That's when I noticed them...the Jet Skis. Oh my, they want us to ride these? I haven't ridden one since the lake, a couple of years ago.

"Elle, are you okay with this?" I asked a little too nervously. "Don't you think we've had enough excitement for a few days?"

"Awe, come on Reese. It will be fun to let loose a little." Then she put her arm through mine and we traipsed up the beach. She really was an awesome best friend. She was SO happy having Finn here too. The guys were walking behind us.

"Now that is a gorgeous site," said Finn. "The two most beautiful girls on the beach are with us. But...I hate to say it...

hearts will be breaking everywhere, because now we get to drown 'em." He laughed out loud as did Tate.

"We'll see about that boys." I said as Elle and I took off running to the jet skis to get to them before the guys did.

"We're driving first," I said getting excited about riding. I had forgotten how much I loved to ride. But, I had also forgotten how much of a wedgy I kept while riding. I couldn't keep my bathing suit bottoms out of *there*. Tate of course loved the back view he had, especially when I was driving. Men!

Maura and Chloe joined us in the water, when we got back. We were having a blast, we had to re-apply sunblock at least twice. I of course enjoyed rubbing it all over Tate's muscular shoulders and back. He and Finn loved watching us girls lather each other up. Like I said...men!

When it was time to go in, I was ready to crash for a while. When I finally got back to the house, and checked my phone for the day, I had two texts and a missed call from Carter.

> Reese, I need to talk with you.
>
> Would you please call me?
>
> –Carter

> I'm worried about you. Call me.
>
> –Carter

I quickly stepped outside to text him back, I was hoping to not have to call him with Tate here.

Carter, I'm fine, I hope you are.

Just hanging out at the beach.

We'll catch up soon.

– R

Within in a few seconds my phone was ringing. Ugh, what should I do? Tate was in the shower, so I answered it. "Hello"

"Reese, thank God. What is going on with you?"

"Hey, to you too. But, um I don't know what you mean. I'm fine." Had he heard about last night? What was this about?

Then he asked, "I mean why are you with Tate? I thought y'all were still broken up. Has something changed?"

"How do you...Why are you...?" I let out a long exhale. "I know it seems crazy, but he ended up driving to Emerald Isle to see me. We had a long talk. I..." Then I just blurted it out, "he didn't sleep with your Mom Carter..." I cringed talking about that to him. "He said it almost got out of hand, but that they never did more than kiss...and touch a little," oh man this did feel weird talking to him about this. "I'm sorry to be talking about it...Tate says your Mom has had a really hard time with your Dad, you know, and that she just needed someone to lean on, and talk too. I guess things got a little carried away." Then I became really curious for why he was so worried. "Besides, how did you know...I mean about Tate?"

Silence on the other end.

Then the sliding glass door opened. Tate was standing in the door frame. "Reese, who are you talking to? Is everything okay?"

"Is that Tate? He's there with you now? I couldn't understand the pictures of y'all on Facebook. But now I get it. He's lying to you Reese. Don't be a fool," he exhaled hard. "I thought we were going to try to work on things when you got back. You know, spend some time together."

I was torn on what to do. I needed to finish this conversation with Carter, but Tate was standing in front of me shirtless, with freshly toweled hair and Nike gym shorts hanging... just so. I could smell the clean soap scent and aftershave from across the porch. Oh my. This was my man. Carter, you missed your chance. "I have to go Carter. I'll call you later....okay?" Then I clicked END. I couldn't take my eyes off of Tate.

"What did he want Reese?" Tate seethed.

I let out a long sigh. "He saw a picture of us on Facebook. He was curious what was going on. I mean the last he heard we were broken up." I made a mental note to thank my friends for that recently posted picture. ugh..

"Of course he thought we were broken up, he orchestrated our break-up," Tate said.

"I know you think that...but it doesn't matter." I walked over to him and placed my hands gently on his sun glistened chest. Then I raised up on my tiptoes, and kissed him ever so lightly. He immediately kissed me back. Then our kiss deepened. Our bodies smashed together. With the setting sun, the feeling was heavenly. Our breathing quickened. Somehow I ended up with my back against the deck railing.

"Tate," I said between kisses.

"Hmmm"

"We need to go in and order pizza."

"Hmmm"

"Tate," Oh my, his hands were traveling up my shirt. I quickly pulled back. My eyes wide like saucers. "Tate, we shouldn't be doing this. They might can see us through all of those windows," I whispered. Our foreheads were touching. We were still trying to catch our breath.

"Okay?" I said.

"Okay," he said reluctantly. "Wait, Reese." He caught my arm as I was walking off. When I turned to look at him his expression was questionable. "Do you love me?" he asked.

"Tate Justice," I said slinking up to him "I couldn't love you more than I do right now." With that we kissed again, then I pulled back, "Why would you need to ask?" "I just want to know you are mine Reese. You could have any guy you want...I mean take your pick..." He threw his hands around like there were twenty guys standing around, "but I need to know you want me...I can't always wonder..."

I knew that was an issue for Tate. In some ways his jealous, possessiveness, was a turn-on and in some ways, it was a little worrisome. I knew he would have to have all of me. I was sure it wouldn't be a problem though, I was his body and soul (at least once we are married, and I just had a crazy feeling one day we would be).

The days flew by. We had an amazing week. Maura and Chloe even had a blast meeting a few new guys on the beach during the day. The guys all tossed the football around. Us girls spent time gossiping and sunning. We even took time to finish a novel, and argue about how it should have really been written. I was getting so attached to having Tate around. He slept in the room with Finn, but every morning he was up before I was, bringing in a fresh cup of coffee to my room. How did I get so lucky? He made me call my mom every day. He said he knew if I was his daughter (uh, let's hope not), he would want to know I was safe. She had been happy with the news of Tate and me getting back together. Of course she grilled me every time we talked, to keep our boundaries, and not regret our time at the beach, if I knew what she meant. Yeah, I knew. I was thankful for those talks. God knows it was so hard. She even went as far as to talk to Elle about reminding me of the values I was raised with. Of course, Elle did it in a funny way every time she caught Tate and me kissing. Tate spent most of his time throwing pillows at her. Little did my Mom know, I was having to give Elle the same advice about her and Finn. Elle was just as happy as I was though. I couldn't think of a better situation, unless of course, Maura and Chloe were dating their brothers.

Carter texted once. I think he was biding his time until I got back home, and away from the beach...*and* away from Tate. I would have to handle that when it was time.

The last night the guys were with us before they went back home had finally arrived. They decided to grill out steaks. The girls all cooked in the kitchen. We had corn on the cob, baked potatoes, and salad. A couple of other guys Maura and Chloe had met were eating with us as well. We even opened a bottle of wine. It was an amazingly clear, warm night with a star show above us. I don't think the evening could have been more perfect. Being Friday night, the star show turned into a fireworks show on the beach. Amazing!

You could hardly see the bruises on my face or body anymore. Tate seemed even happier that he didn't have that constant reminder to look at. After we were through eating and cleaning up, Tate and I took a long walk on the beach.

Then we came back in and watched TV in my room. We decided we wanted to be alone, since I would have plenty of time with the girls (at least five more days) once he and Finn were gone. Tate was heading home in the morning, gathering his stuff, and going straight to baseball training at Wake Forest. I would have to spend too long missing him then.

We were laying on top of the covers his front to my back. It felt so right with him holding me close. His breath warm on my neck. We were deep into watching Rambo. He loved those movies, so I surprised him with it on pay-per-view. I didn't care for the blood and guts, but I loved Tate, and I wouldn't see him for a while after tomorrow. So I sucked it up.

About halfway through the movie, he started kissing on the back of my neck and rubbing his nose on my ear. The feel of his uneven, jagged breaths at the base of my scalp sent tingles everywhere. My body was definitely hyper aware of what was happening.

I whispered "Tate, you're going to miss the movie."

I got no response. He just continued nuzzling on my neck. His hands were around my waist, his fingers kneading my sides. Then, he turned me towards him. The look in his eyes was smoldering.

I said "Tate, we have to be careful, we can't get too carried away."

"Hmmm, we will be...careful," he said, kissing my cheek.

I was praying he was right.

Then our lips were caressing each others...soft, slow, tender. My lips were parted by his tongue, exploring mine. Oh, the feeling of kissing the man I loved, the man who wanted me, and protected me was...exquisite. I was lost in the moment.

His hands were traveling up my shirt gently massaging my breasts. He pulled back the top of my bra and lowered his head to kiss the nipple of my left breast. I had never let anyone, willingly, do that. It felt...wonderful, my body quaked all over. I felt strange aches from down low, the good kind of aches. He slowly circled his tongue over and over. The rhythmic sensation caused me to push my pelvis into his. I can't begin to describe the feeling. Then his mouth found mine again, and we were kissing like we would never see each other again.

"You are mine Reese," he said. "I promise to always take care of you." Of course I knew these words from him. He had said them so many times before. But he had never said them while we were doing...this, making out so, intense. This time those words meant even more.

"Always," I said. My teeth grabbed his lower lip before I pushed my tongue back in his mouth and he let out a low moan, as did I. Then his hands slid down and pulled up my sundress. He rubbed on the back of my upper thighs, slowly working his way to my front. He slid my panties to the side, my heart ready to explode, and he gently touched me *there*. My body was pushing up against his hand instinctively. I was no longer controlled by my mind, just my body. His body had changed in a matter of seconds. I could feel the hardness of him pushing into my side, as our bodies meshed together.

He was rubbing, circling, exploring. I wasn't breathing. I think I temporarily forgot how. He, on the other hand, was breathing hard enough for both of us. With his other hand, he was gently caressing my nipple, then ever so lightly pinching it between his fingers. I had a rush of heat throughout my body.

I felt like I would nearly combust. His lips were teasing my ear, sending sensations from my head to my toes. Oh God…

Tate spoke my name. When I opened my eyes he had his locked on mine. My heavy eyelids were stealing the intensity of his look. I barely recognized he was talking to me "Reese, can…" All of a sudden my brain kicked in. I quickly pushed his hand away and put my forehead to his.

"I can't Tate." There was a long pause. You could only hear our breathing. "I'm sorry, but I can't." I barely got the words out of my mouth. I think I was still floating above the bed too.

"No, I'm sorry…I didn't mean to get that far Reese. I never want you to regret anything we do together," he said as he hugged me.

My heart was still racing. "I know. We…we got carried away. I want to do the right thing though Tate. I want us to wait…can we? Can you…wait? I knew this was torture for him too. I could only imagine the physical issues it was causing him to not act in the moment. He was painfully quiet. "Do you see this ring Tate? My parents gave it to me when I turned 13. It's called a promise ring…a promise to them, and to God and to my future husband, that I will wait until I'm married." I let out a long sigh. "Like I said, I want to do the right thing, but why would something that feels so right be so wrong? And, why would God have to make us so…sensitive, to…touch and feelings," I raised my eyebrows at Tate and looked down between us, "and not want us to act on them?"

"It's okay Reese. I get it. I promise. I will wait for you. You need to be married first, right? Well, let's just make a plan to see that happen in the future…me and you…now YOU promise me that." I shook my head yes…with that, he kissed me. Not the sensual moment from before, but the passion of a promise.

# CHAPTER 22

The morning came too quickly. Tate made me coffee as usual, but this time I had woken up before him and fixed him a full course breakfast: egg and cheese omelets, bacon, toast, grits, and fruit. Of course, I made enough for all of us including Finn's hearty appetite. Maura and Chloe had slept in, after they had hung out late with their new 'friends'. Just the four of us were sitting in the kitchen. We were talking about what baseball was going to be like. I was starting to get SO sad thinking about Tate being gone. I wouldn't see him for almost three weeks. Elle and I would be without our boys for much too long. Luckily, we'd have a few weeks of summer left before I had to head off to Wake too.

They left around 10 am so they could drive back and get packed. They wanted to spend a little time with family, before leaving Sunday morning. They would have to leave around 6 am for Wake Forest. Tate hadn't been gone 10 minutes before he texted me.

Reese, last night was..amazing. you and me = future.

I'll think about you everyday... in that way ;) Love and miss you already.

Tate

I was so lucky to have this man. So lucky that we were going to school together in the fall and according to Chloe's note on my pillow last night, so lucky that he was heading home today. I was still laughing at her note. She had written: Dad is finally heading home in the morning...time to PARTY! I laughed out loud thinking about it. She felt like Tate and Finn were crimping our girl time.

Although more tamed than the first two nights at the beach, the night Tate left was great. I love my girlfriends. And well, girls will be girls. We dolled up and went dancing. I love to dance and with my black eye, I had felt I couldn't go the whole week Tate was here. But now, it had faded enough that make-up covered up the rest. We went to a local club at Atlantic Beach. I wasn't interested in 'hooking up' at all, of course. But, I would still tell Tate I had gone. I would want to know if he went, after all. We danced most of the night. I felt like I had lost five pounds before we left.

As we were heading out the door, a bouncer handed me an envelope. I was leery to open it. I mean who gets a 'note' at a dance club? But when I did, my breath caught. The note said: Please accept this gift.

You deserve it after all you've been through...John. There was a gift certificate to Lameen's Spa and Resort for $1,000. Oh my God. Was he crazy? The girls were eyeing me like they were getting ready to fight whoever left me the note. Then they jumped up and down when I told them. There was even a date and time for tomorrow...11 am (good we could still sleep in). It even said transportation would be provided.

"Hell yeah!" said Chloe. "I knew his money would come in handy. He feels guilty and we benefit!!"

"Wait," I said feeling...bought. "I don't think I can accept this...I mean what would Tate say?"

"Why would Tate even know...Reese? Who is going to tell him?" She gave me the BIG eyes like 'if you know what's best, you won't'.

I ignored her. "Look, I know this would be fun...but..."

"But...it's okay Reese. Tate really doesn't need to know who paid for our pampering, just maybe that we went," said Elle.

"Exactly," said Maura.

Oh good grief. My friends were ganging up on me here.

"Okay...I guess we could go for..." before I could get the rest out, they all jumped on me hugging me and squealing. It was going to be fun. I just hope I wouldn't have to pay later...whatever that means...for accepting such an extravagant gift.

"Hey, doesn't it bother any of you that he knew we were here..." I said looking around like I was trying to find him.

"Now that I think of it, yes, it does. But, if he were too 'stalkish', he would pop out...right...now!" said Chloe slowly and she jumped with her hands out like she had just scared us.

We all laughed. I still thought it was a little crazy though.

The next day we were so excited to be getting spa treatments. We were all ready by 10:45 am when we heard a horn beep. In some way I was expecting it to be John. And in some ways I was disappointed when it was a driver and a limousine...a Limo! Everyone screamed. I did too. But then my conscience piped up...was this right? Why couldn't this be for Maura or any of the girls...Uhh. I wasn't sure what the right thing was... well actually, I knew it would be to not accept this gift, but my girlfriends were so excited. I had to allow them that. Right?

⌒⌒

The spa was amazing! We each had massages and facials. We sat in the sauna (that was scary...women of all 'sizes' sitting in there nude...we were in robes). The spa provided white, fluffy robes, and fresh lemons in water. We wore cucumbers on our eyes. We even sat in the planetarium room with the pretend stars over-head, and strange outside noises on surround sound. We laid in lounge chairs that leaned back making our feet elevated. Chloe of course, made crazy moves with her legs like scissors the whole time, and then pretending like she was...um...you know. We laughed until we cried. We were supposed to be relaxing!!

I would say we had a wonderful time. After we were all dressed, and donned new make-up, provided in the plush bathrooms, we headed outside. The limo was still waiting on us. We got in, but the driver wasn't going toward home, he was heading in the opposite direction. We pulled up to a fancy restaurant in Morehead City. This time John was waiting for us... John, Harrison, Kerry and Brett. *Brett*...I was all of a sudden nervous and upset. And just after my relaxing spa treatments too.

"Chloe, you promised," I said.

She leaned over and grabbed my hand, "I still do Reese. I won't ever do that again okay?" That was the serious Chloe I never see, but I knew she meant it. Just as quickly, she was wild and crazy again. "But we can still have fun!!" she said looking like Santa Claus had just arrived...I don't know, maybe he had.

We all got out. I was the last one, unsure of the lines I was crossing.

"Reese..." John leaned in and kissed my cheek.

"John, I can't believe you did all of this." I said pointing to the limo.

"I was afraid you would say no...I'm so glad you didn't," said John.

"I wouldn't have gone, if my friends hadn't been so excited. That was too much John."

"No way. Besides, I needed another way to say I'm sorry."

"I've told you, I forgive you." I said looking at him as genuine as I could.

"Reese, I can do this...and much more...please let me."

I wasn't sure what he meant by much more, but it scared me. I would have to be really strong to continue to be faithful to Tate, but I was determined.

"Before I forget," I said. "I've been thinking about Sam."

He furrowed his brow at me. "Please, don't. I can't bear for you to say his name after what he tried to do to you."

"I mean, I've been thinking what I...we...can do to keep him from doing this to someone else. If he hadn't been stopped... he would've raped me John."

He looked like he'd been crushed. "I know...don't remind me..." he let out a long breath... "I think he's taken care of for a while. I've admitted him to a drug rehab program for several weeks. After that, he'll be monitored daily by his father...his worst nightmare."

I will admit that made me feel a little better.

"Okay, I guess you have it covered. I just pray I never learn that another girl has been taken advantage of by him." I said quietly. The thought of him brought up so many vivid memories.

"Hey, let's go in and eat. I bet after all of that pampering, you're starved," he said with a half-grin. He led me inside with his hand on my back. I wondered if we looked like a couple. I prayed we didn't.

Dinner was amazing. The girls had a great time. I grilled Brett as did Elle and Maura on his behavior. He claims Sam gave him the cocaine, and that he'd only done it one other time, during college. They rode with us home. I thanked John for a wonderful day and evening. I also reminded him that I was with Tate. He said he knew, of course, and that we were just destined to be close friends. Brett and Harrison had already worked up hanging out on the beach tomorrow. I wasn't sure how I agreed to that one, but in the end, I said I would see him tomorrow.

Day after day they came and hung out with us at the beach. They were so much fun. I enjoyed the laughs and the exercise for sure. They loved football and corn-hole. I had to just be careful with the tackling. It seemed John liked that part the best. If I say I loved spending time with John, it would be a serious understatement. The man was a true gentleman, and so damn fine.

By the last day, Chloe and Maura were eating up every minute with 'their guys'. I know, I had been there recently and so had Elle. The difference was Elle and I would see our guys again soon, but Maura and Chloe might not see theirs again... ever, at least not for a long, long time.

That day we stayed on the beach until nearly 6 pm. Then we parted ways. I decided to go home with the girls the next day and not stay by myself at the beach as I had planned. I wasn't in that dark place I had been when I arrived, so I didn't seem to need that 'alone' time. Not long after they left we showered and dressed, then packed. I loved this place, Elle's beach house. I loved the serenity of the beach itself. It's probably my favorite place to be. As I was sitting out on the porch reminiscing over my time here, I heard someone coming up the steps.

John.

"John...what are you doing here?" I asked. I hope I didn't come across as rude, but I was surprised to see him again.

John seemed a little tense. "I couldn't let you leave yet. I wanted to see you once more."

h no. Not this. This gorgeous, beach god was standing in front of me telling me he didn't want me to go yet.

"Before you speak, I just wanted you to know how much I will miss you...how much I care for you," he said walking up to me, and sitting beside of me in another rocker on the porch.

"John, I'm with Tate...nothing will change that...but I have enjoyed getting to know you better...really, I have." I tried to sound genuine without sounding like I wanted him 'that' way. I was so confused by my emotions. I just really needed him to not be around. I knew deep in my gut that if I weren't with Tate, I would be with this endearing man, John.

He looked straight at me. "That's what you keep telling me," he chuckled. "I know you're with Tate. I know y'all have a history Reese. I just think you're amazing. I want to keep in touch with you...I need to know that's okay."

I hesitated. I wondered how I would feel if this was some girl asking Tate the same question. Some girl he met at Myrtle Beach before we made up. I'd be really jealous, and probably a little hurt too. But was this different? I mean this was John. We'd been through so much together already.

"Um, I guess so. I mean, I guess it's okay. Sure...we can keep in touch. We are friends after all," I said.

He reached over and grabbed my hand. I flinched but his hand felt too good in mine. I was desperately thinking in my head...Tate, why did you have to leave? I'm too weak to be near John. I had KISSED this man just over a week ago...I mean really kissed, and had really enjoyed it too.

John must have sensed what I was feeling. He began rubbing my hand with his thumb.

"Reese, can I just hug you once more. I mean, we'll stay in touch...but us actually touching...I mean hugging might not happen...again." God, why did he have to be so damn gorgeous?

John, I'm not sure" I looked over at his hand on mine. "You're holding my hand already. That's almost crossing the line as it is."

He stood up and held his other hand out to me. I hesitated for another moment, then he pulled me out of my chair and put his arms around me.

"Oh Reese. I don't want you to leave tomorrow. I want us to stay just like this."

Shit! I needed to be strong...I needed to be strong. Maybe if I kept repeating this mantra, I could be.

"John. Why didn't you meet another girl while you were here? Someone to REALLY spend your time with and get to know better. Once you knew Tate and I were back together, you should have done that," I said. Although I was silently thankful that he hadn't for some selfish reason, I know. Now we weren't only hugging we were swaying...dancing to Elle's iPod. She had left it out on the deck. She had my mom's and her mom's songs on there too, like mine. Bon Jovi's song, 'I'll Be There For You' was playing. We were silent for a couple of minutes. He was so warm and smelled so good. His head was in the crook of my neck. I was worried he would kiss my skin. I was worried about how much I wanted him to at that moment. I was feeling a little too comfortable in his arms.

Then, he said "Reese, I know you think I'm crazy for...well for being so crazy over you so quick. But, I am. I've never felt this way about anyone. I wish you weren't back with Tate...I'll blame myself for that. But I want you to know...I. Will. Wait. For. You." He said with entirely too much passion.

I started to talk, but he put his hand up to my mouth.

"I will. I will wait. I have this feeling that it won't be long. It won't be long before you and Tate are apart again."

I was sure I had this pained look behind his hand. I reached up and pulled his hand down. "I'm sorry you think that John. But, I think we're in it to stay."

He only smiled at me then, and wrapped his arms tighter around me. He leaned back and lifted my chin to stare into his eyes. I couldn't describe the intensity I saw there. We locked eyes for several moments. I was afraid he would bend down and kiss me. My heart was racing. All of this was wrong on so many levels. Finally, he whispered goodbye, and left. I wasn't sure what I was feeling at his departure - relief, regret, I wasn't sure. The one thing I was sure of was, that wasn't the last I would hear from him. There was a definite part of my heart that was happy with that. But, I was already worried for the questions I would have to answer from Tate.

The morning we left, we walked out to my jeep and there was a gift bag in the seat. I knew it had to be from John. With it was a note that read:

Dear Reese,

I promise this is not the end. I'll be in touch...soon. But until then, know ..I.....Will....Wait.

Love,
John

P.S just like the song," I'll be there for you" right when you need me.

Inside the bag were gift certificates to various places. As I sorted through them I found they were to all the places we pass by on the way home. Starbucks for breakfast, Panera for lunch, and Outback for supper. Then there were gift cards to Barnes and Nobles, Dillards, JCrew, and Sephora. All places we had talked about this week. At the bottom of the bag was a box that contained a brand new **iPhone**. Oh my God. I can't believe he gave me an iPhone. On the back of the box was a note that read...*replace that old flip phone of yours Reese. This way we can stay better connected*. What? I was sure that wasn't a good idea. I let out a long breath. I turned on the new phone and started playing around with it. When I went to the music icon, he had downloaded all of the songs we had listened to since the first time he met me. He had thought of everything.

I really didn't want my friends to see any of it, but Chloe peeked over my shoulder shaking her head saying, "if only I had whatever aura you release Reese, I could be a rich woman!! Love 'em and leave 'em I say." She was laughing but then she told Maura and Elle. Elle looked concerned as she came over to me.

"Reese, be careful. I know you love Tate, but I think John has his sights set on you. He doesn't seem to care that you're with Tate...just...be careful. Even the strongest person couldn't withstand some of his tactics, not to mention his gorgeous looks."

I knew she was right. I would have to make an effort to just stay away from him in the future. The problem was he was used to getting what he wanted it seems, and as far as I knew that had never been a girl until now...wasn't I lucky. I let out another long breath, silently shaking my head.

# CHAPTER 23

The ride home was made even better with all of our...uh... my free gifts. On the way home, I stopped by the phone store and had my new phone activated. Halfway home, my phone pinged.

> Reese, I hope you found my gifts. I want to do so much more for you. I hope you'll let me. I can show you the world, you know.
>
> I'll be in touch soon.
>
> Love – J

Elle, could see the confused look on my face when I read the text. She leaned over to me and said. "Girl, what are you going to do? I mean, what is he thinking? So, he has money and he's gorgeous. Does he think you're just going to leave Tate because of that?"

"I'm not sure what he thinks. He keeps saying he will wait for me, like Tate and I will be over one day. I'm not sure, but I think he feels we are destined to be together for some reason. I just have to hope that time and space changes his mind..." I said.

"Do you Reese? I mean how do you really feel about him? I can't imagine having to have his constant texts, and money, and blue eyes, and strong jaw, and cut arms, and jet black hair, and..."

"Elle! You're not helping here! What in the world." I all but yelled.

"I'm sorry." She chuckled out loud. "I got carried away. Anyway, at least you have a back-up plan, and a damn good one too, if you and Tate do break up. I don't know of any other girls in your position."

Of course it wasn't long before Maura and Chloe caught on to what we were talking about. Maura agreed it would be hard to have my dilemma too.

But as usual, Chloe had a different, unique perspective. "I think you're just a trashy whore Reese." She laughed out loud, "I mean Carter is pining away for you in Penderton, hoping you will give him another chance. Tate thinks you walk on water, and wants you to be his wife, and drop his babies. And John, well he thinks you should be his muse, so he can buy you everything he comes across. I say the hell with all of them. And, damn it, why don't you just share them with us? Who needs that many men anyhow? I'm sure you could get rid of all three today, and find an even better, more willing participant tomorrow! After all, you just have that way Reese." Chloe said. She was laughing, but I could tell she was a little serious too.

"Chloe, are you mad? I mean don't be hatin'. I didn't ask for this. Life isn't always this grand for me either, I..."

"She knows that Reese," said Elle, cutting me off. "She's just jealous."

I'm not sure why Elle felt a need to interrupt. I guess she thought I would tell about the date rape, but I wasn't ready for that yet. I loved my friends, but I just wasn't ready....

"I am. I'll admit it....I'm jealous. I guess maybe if I would learn to hold back from guys a little more, maybe I would get some of the chances you get Reese." There was a long pause. "But, listen, I'm sorry, you do have a true issue with John. He's amazing and all. But, if you're not careful, he'll drive a wedge between you and Tate. Tate has the whole package, like I said before, but as rich as he is, he can't compete with moneybags. Guys don't like to be outdone...I'm just saying."

I was quiet for a while. As usual, Chloe was dead on. I knew they were all right. But without getting downright ugly with John, I didn't know how else I could tell him, I was with Tate. A selfish part of me didn't want to. I knew that. Maybe that was what was keeping me feeling really nervous all of the time. I let out a long sigh.

"Well, I appreciate all of your insight. God knows I can use all of the advice I can get. I love you all, and I'm so glad we had these past two weeks together." We all did a group hug. I don't know what I would do without my friends.

By the time I had dropped them all off, and said our good-byes, I was exhausted, and ready to hug my Mom and Dad. It was SO great to see them. My Dad helped me carry my bags in, then they both wanted me to sit in the living room to fill them all in. I told them how I had met John the first night we got there, and how after Tate and I had gotten back together, he still wanted to see me. My dad gave me a warning lecture about how Tate was bound to not want another guy trying to bide for my time. (Oh Dad, if you only knew). Later, Mom and I had a heart to heart about Tate. She thinks we are in it for the long haul...like her and Dad were. I hope she's right. She also said that Carter was dying to see me and how Lisa was secretly hoping we got back together (Oh, I'm sure she was). I didn't bother to tell either one of them about Sam. That part of my life will be forever closed...thankfully.

I knew it wouldn't be long before I heard from Carter. And I was right. He called the day after I got back, and asked if he could come over and hang out at my house. I told him I didn't think it was a good idea, that Tate was out of town, and he wouldn't appreciate it. The next day he showed up anyway. I'll admit a part of my heart still beats erratically when he was around. He has always had that effect on me. I guess it's the history we shared. He was a handsome guy with a big personality. I once upon a time thought I was in love with him, after all.

I insisted on being in our family room, sitting in different chairs while he stayed. We watched an episode of Survivor, then he wanted to talk. He told me all about his rehab and how he was improving, but he was pretty sure he wouldn't be able to run track for UNC. His academic scholarship was granted however, since his sports scholarship was on hold. I was glad to hear that, but I was sorry to hear he would no longer be running. I knew how much he enjoyed that...it seemed to be a good outlet for him. At least it seemed to keep him sidetracked enough to stay apart from me when he left before.

"Reese, I was really hoping I would be here for more than 'catching up'. I was hoping at this stage, that we would be back together." Oh no, here we go.

"Carter, I don't really…"

"I know you don't see us that way now," he cut me off "but I only wish I hadn't been so STUPID to not call you, and see you enough when I left last year. I was just SO messed up in the head."

I was getting a little worried, his voice was escalating, and he seemed really upset. Then he came over and sat, actually he squeezed in beside of me in the over-sized chair I was sitting in.

"I was Reese. I was stupid. I can't believe how bad I withdrew last year. I really missed you." His voice was different, and he was gazing at me like I would change my mind if I looked at him. So I kept my eyes on the floor until he reached over and grabbed my hand, bringing it to his mouth and kissing it. That of course made my eyes shoot to his. Then he got up, looking back at me he walked halfway towards the door and said. "I won't push you Reese. I almost died in that crash, it made me realize everything I was missing in my life."

I still didn't say anything. My eyes were focused on my hands in my lap.

"By the way, I talked with my Mom. She wouldn't tell me about anything with Tate. I think she didn't want to hurt me. But, I'm sure she had an affair with him. He's lying to you Reese. I can't believe you don't see it. I'll just have to prove it to you." And with that he walked out.

I tried my best to enjoy the rest of June and first part of July even though Tate was still gone. I spent a lot of time at the pool. Since I had been a lifeguard for the past two summers, they let me work a few hours here and there to make some extra spending money. One day, I was sitting in the lifeguard stand, twirling my whistle, and watching the cute little kids playing around in the pool. I heard a group of my age girls walk by, kind of whispering. My back was to them, so I couldn't make out exactly who it was at first, but I heard them say 'Tate'. I wondered what they would by saying about my boyfriend, so I listened. I heard "Tate is being scouted by the pros because of my dad, and they plan to bring him to a tryout this coming fall." I wasn't sure yet who had said it, but I was sure they were talking about my Tate. I mean we live in a small town, and I didn't know another Tate. As soon as the group of girls had gone by, I scoped out who they were. It was Lauren Taylor and her group of catty girls in their teeny bikinis. Why did she have to have a history with my man? Chloe said that she was wanting him back again, and that she was ruthless. I wasn't worried about Tate falling for her, but I was worried about what she would do to try and attain him. I would have to ask him what she could be talking about...the pros? That was like nothing I had heard of for Tate before now. I mean, I knew he was awesome at baseball, but the pros? Only time would tell, I guess. I would've really liked to have called Tate and asked him about it, but he was pretty much inaccessible at camp. My long conversations would have to happen once we were face to face. I couldn't wait.

I was able to save a little money through working, although, my mom wouldn't let me use it for shopping with her. She successfully spoiled me every way possible. Being her only child, a daughter no less, and now I was going away for college - I could feel the empty nest syndrome coming on for her and my dad. I walked with my mom most evenings around the neighborhood. We talked about how much life had changed since she was my age, and what it was like for her going away to college. Her two brothers were younger, so my Grandparents didn't experience the emotions like her.

My mom got teary many nights just talking about me leaving. There were a couple of times we got to talking about Lisa, and I wanted to tell my mom so bad about her and Tate. But I just couldn't. I knew if she ever knew, she and my dad might think of him differently. And I was sure she would think of Lisa differently. My mom loved her and would need all of her friends to help keep her company when I was gone.

I also spent a lot of time with 'the girls'. Although Elle would be my roommate at WF, I wouldn't see Maura or Chloe as often. So, the four of us went to the lake some, and spent time in the cabin too...lots of time in the cabin. We reminisced and looked at pictures through the years. God, we were hideous in our early teens...braces can be scary.

Carter had texted me some, but surprisingly I hadn't heard from John. I figured it was best that way. However, I did wonder if he had maybe moved on. I was sure there were girls at every turn trying to get his attention. It was strange really. I had honestly felt a deep connection to him, and in such a short amount of time. I wasn't sure what to make of it. I knew if Tate and I hadn't gotten back together, I would probably be getting even closer with John. That's how much I enjoyed being with him. But, that wasn't in the plans. Tate and I did get back together, and I'd never want to hurt him. So, needless to say, it was best if I never heard from John again.

———

I was getting excited to see Tate. On the day he was supposed to return, I had a special night planned for us. Of course we had talked each night briefly, but we also texted a lot, and I was following the team's schedule for practice and scrimmage through their website and on Facebook. I knew we would have a lot to talk about when he got home. I couldn't wait to hear what he thought campus life would be like. I spent the day at the pool, and was heading home to get ready when my phone pinged.

It was John.

I couldn't believe he hadn't texted me in nearly two weeks and then the night I'm to meet with Tate, he texts me.

> Reese, I'm coming through your town on my way to Raleigh for business. Can I see you? I have a premonition Tate will screw up and you'll need me to 'be there for you'. ;)
>
> –J

What in the world am I supposed to say to that? I can't see him, it wouldn't be right. And, what premonition is he talking about. I texted him back.

> John, it was great to hear from you. It's been a while. I was wondering if you were able to move

on already. I wish you the best, but I don't think
it's a good idea if we meet.

–Reese

For some reason, I felt bad for the text I'd sent him. He made
me feel so important to him, and I was just so…casual. I hoped
he wasn't mad, but I have to do what Tate would expect. After my
shower, I dressed in Tate's favorite navy sundress, and I slipped
in the diamond hairpin he loved so much. I had a picnic ready to
take to Lookout Ledge. It was a cool, private hangout up on the
mountain that overlooked the town below. Back in the 50's it was
a drive-in movie theatre. Now, on warm nights, it was a perfect
place to take a picnic basket and chill out under the stars. I had
my blanket in the jeep, my iPod, and the food. I was ready to go.
I looked down at my phone and realized that I had received my
third text of the day from Carter. I guess he was worried over Tate
coming back into town. This last text simply said.

I need to see you, let's meet at our old, special
place 7:30pm.

–Carter

What? Carter no. I can't…then it dawned on me where
that place was. I don't know why I hadn't thought of it before.
Carter and I had our first kiss at Lookout Ledge. Surely he
doesn't mean there. I have to stop this, I thought.

I can't Carter.

Not tonight. Maybe tomorrow or another day, okay?

–Reese

I didn't hear back from him before it was time for me to meet with Tate. So I prayed that he wouldn't crash our mini reunion tonight. I didn't want to share my evening with Tate with anyone. I figured since he didn't text back, he was happy that I might see him tomorrow.

The time had finally arrived. I drove up to our spot, and when I got there Tate was already leaning up against his truck, waiting on me. Oh my, my man was fine. He had on a Nike Sports, tight-fitting shirt with khaki shorts and tennis shoes. He was a sight to behold. His tanned, chiseled arms were crossed in front of him. His smile widened as he saw me pull in. I couldn't wait to be in his arms. I got out and before I could turn around, he was wrapping his arms around me.

"Mmmm, you feel amazing. I'm so glad you're here," said Tate.

I turned to face him giving him a quick peck. Then I pulled back and looked into his eyes. "I believe you are even more handsome, Tate. I bet the girls were falling all over you there." We hugged tighter. I blushed. I wasn't used to giving compliments like that. But, it was true. He was divine.

"I have a feeling I'm not the one with the stories. I'm reluctant to ask if you heard from Carter since I've been gone," said Tate.

I wasn't about to spoil our first evening with talk about Carter, much less about my time with John (although innocent) back at the beach after he left. "Nothing sizzling to report here." I winked up at him. "I'm still 100% yours." then I quickly looked away and said, "I've got us a picnic basket of food. I hope you're hungry?"

He reached over and grabbed me, swiftly pulling me up to him. "Oh I'm hungry all right. I'm dying for one of these..." He bent down and kissed me hard and tender at the same time. I could feel the love radiating from his lips. Then he deepened it, making me blush. I wasn't about to pull away.

But, finally he did. "Hey Reese, I meant to ask you, did you get a new phone?" I froze up real quick. Well, yeah, but how would you already know that, I thought.

"Why do you ask?"

"Well, I got a text from you earlier, but it was a different number than usual."

"How could that happen, I haven't changed my number?" I was getting a little weirded out, "What did it say?"

"It said to meet you up here at 7:30. So I figured when I talked with you earlier and you said 7, that you had changed your mind. But I was planning to ask you about the number you texted from."

Just then we saw a car drive up and end our intimate privacy. The phone number issue put to the back burner for now. Hopefully whoever it was wouldn't stay long. It would be nice to have our picnic with no one else around. But just as the car was parking, I realized our night had taken a drastic turn. It was Carter.

Tate was fuming mad. "Did he know we were coming here Reese? Is that why he's here? I guess it's time I had a few words with him...again."

As Carter got out and walked towards us my heart was racing. I wasn't sure what was going to happen, but the last time these two were together they were fighting. This time my dad wasn't here to break them up. All of a sudden I was finding it hard to breathe. Before Tate could speak, I started walking toward Carter until I felt a hand pulling me back. Tate's eyes were wild with anger. He stared at me and said, "No Reese, it's time I took care of this."

Somehow I slowly nodded, completely unsure of what I really should do.

"Carter, why are you here?" Tate fumed.

"Not for you, I can promise you that," said Carter. Then he turned to me as if Tate wasn't there and said "Reese I knew you would come." He literally had a peaceful smile across his features. "I'm so glad you did. Now we can tell Tate how we really feel okay? It will be nice to get the truth out about him and my mom too," he was holding out his hand to me.

Then it dawned on me what was happening. He came here hoping by chance that I would show up at our 'special place'. I was sure me telling him that I couldn't see him would have been enough for him to know I wouldn't come. He had no idea we would be here though...me and Tate. I felt sure of that, but not sure of anything else at that moment.

"Wait, Carter, I didn't come here for you. Tate and I had already planned to be here." I was trying to speak slowly and clearly, but inside I was freaking out.

"Reese, explain this to me, how did he know to come here?" Tate asked.

I let out a frustrated, long breath, but in no way was relaxing. Staring at the ground I said, "he had texted me earlier to meet him tonight...at our special place, but I told him no, I was seeing you tonight. I guess he came up here to make sure I hadn't changed my mind." I looked to Carter for confirmation. His eyes were locked on mine.

"So this is your special place with *him?*" Tate pointed to Carter like he was disgusted at what he was saying.

"Tell him Reese...our first kiss was up here," he whispered, while staring at me, pleading with me to remember. "We held each other and you let me..." Tate cut him off.

"Stop this shit. Reese, why would you want to be up here with me if it meant so much to...to y'all?" Tate was running his hand through his hair trying to calm down...I hoped.

"Tate, wait, we've been up here several times too over the past year." I motioned at Tate and me. "It's just a gorgeous place to spend an evening as a couple. It wasn't that it was so special between Carter and me. I just really like it up here. Please don't look too deep in to this."

"Reese, you don't know what you're saying..." Carter started walking towards me, his eyes still set on mine. "We fell in love up here, you were mine up here..." His eyes were crazy, wild, like I had never seen them.

"Carter, I'm warning you...get the hell out of here." Tate said through clenched teeth.

"Wait..." I looked at Tate trying to put an end to this, then back to Carter. "I don't love you Carter." I was trying my best to get him to understand. "I love Tate. What we had is over. Please leave." Tears were threatening to spill over if I even blinked.

"Reese, we can never be over. I own you body and soul." Then he turned to Tate and spoke slowly and clearly, "You. Can't. Have. Her. I have already taken her Tate. You can never get back what will always be mine forever...her virginity."

My head was spinning. What was he talking about...then the realization and familiarity of his words made my heart stop.

"Carter," I think I was speaking, but I'm not sure if the words were really coming out. "You don't know what you're saying." I pleaded, but he kept walking towards me, then Tate jumped on him, knocking Carter to the ground. I started screaming but I didn't know what to do. I was shuffling around like a crazy person. I was yelling both of their names trying to reason with them to stop, and stupidly trying to get in between them. I caught a glimpse of something shiny in Carter's hand...a Gun!

"Tate, Carter has a gun...oh my God. No!"

*Boom.*

The sound of the shot rang through my ears. I was falling to the ground. My lungs were burning, I couldn't blink my eyes, I couldn't put my hands out to catch myself, I was falling.... My body landed hard on the ground, my head hit something with a thud. I heard Tate screaming my name, and then there was another shot...

*Boom.*

I saw a fuzzy image running out of the woods. Tony, Carter's Dad...what was he?...The next thing I saw was **darkness**........

# CHAPTER 24

Beeping.
Beeping all around.
Faint voices. What was happening? Where was I?
Then darkness....

⌒

Is that you Mom? No, don't cry. Why can't I open my eyes? What's happening to me? Oh God help me....

Total darkness...

⌒

"Her eyes are fluttering. Hey Liz, look, her eyes. She's trying to open them. Reese, wake up honey...we need you to wake up..."

I knew that voice. But I couldn't open my eyes, the light... it was too bright. Please cut off the light. I can't open my eyes. I started to feel my body. My arms were so heavy. Was I under water? My eyelids were stuck. I couldn't swallow, my throat felt like sandpaper.

A touch on my hand. Oh, that I could feel. A tender, soft touch. Now a touch on my other hand.

"Sweetheart...you have to wake up...we have to know..." Crying. That, that was my dad...he's crying. What's wrong with me? No Daddy, I'm okay. I'm here. I just...I just can't open my eyes.

"Excuse me, I need to get over to her please." Who was that? I don't recognize that voice. Ouch. Stop that. It hurts. "I'm just adjusting her chest tube. Looks like the little lady is waking up." I didn't recognize that voice...tube, what does that mean? My head is killing me.

"Ohhh" I groaned. I heard it, I groaned out loud. Didn't I?

"Reese, wake up, please. Show me those gorgeous green eyes baby." Tate...I felt a soft kiss on my cheek.

"Tate..." I croaked.

"Oh thank God...Reese, we're all here...your Mom, Dad, Elle, Chloe, Maura, my parents. We're here. Come on, wake up and talk to us." That was Tate. My Tate....

I fluttered my eyes open a little more..."water"..."I need..."..."water".

"Oh, here honey," I felt a straw touch my lips "drink it slowly okay." That was my Mom and she was crying too.

"Okay." I said and everyone laughed. What was so funny?

"Thank God Reese. You're making sense. We've been worried to death about you," and more crying...that voice was Elle's.

I felt myself smile then slowly opened my eyes trying to adjust to the light all around me.

"What happened? Where am I?" I spoke, but barely. \

"You're in the hospital honey. You...you were in an accident. Do you remember? I'm not sure what to tell you yet...

but, you were shot and hit your head on a rock when you fell," my mom said. I could make out her face now. Oh Mom, I'm sorry I made you worry. You look like you haven't slept in days, I thought.

Slowly what she said sank in...once it registered I gasped out loud and felt around for Tate.

"Oh God Tate, you...were you shot too? Are you okay?" Then that gorgeous face came into view. He too looked like he hadn't slept in days. He had stubble all on his face and his eyes had dark circles underneath.

"I'm okay Reese. I wasn't shot. I almost died worrying about you, but I...I wasn't shot..." he was crying, nearly sobbing. He dropped his forehead to my hand.

Elle walked over behind him and put her hand on Tate's shoulder. "We almost lost you Reese. We've all been going crazy. I...love...you, and I'm so glad you're awake," she said through sobs.

"I'm sorry I scared everyone. I don't know how it happened. What about Carter and his dad? How are they?" I said in a strained voice.

No one spoke.

I was all of a sudden desperate to get some answers "Tate, Carter had a gun. I was scared to death. Is he at home? I imagine he got into a lot of trouble for having a gun when y'all were fighting."

"Reese, Carter...he didn't make it....he was shot in the stomach, and he...he died lying beside of you on the ground... at Lookout Ledge."

"Oh God, no." Oh God, he's wrong isn't he, Carter didn't die? But as I looked around the room all of the eyes I met told the same story. Why God, why did Carter have to die? I looked to my Mom for confirmation. She was looking down at the bed.

"Mom, Lisa and Tony, they must be devastated." I said "I mean for Tony to see his son die like that...Oh God, I can't imagine. Carter...." I was sobbing now. I couldn't believe he was dead. Memories from when we were dating flashed before my eyes...then memories of his last comments made to me.

My eyes flashed to Tate's. "Tate, what he said...we didn't...I promise,"

The look on his face was one of torture. "Reese, I had so much time to think about that..." He looked around the room, "we can talk about that later okay? Trust me...it's okay?"

"And honey, don't worry, Tony was at home with Lisa when Carter died. She called and talked to me about it," my mom said. "They're devastated as is his brother, Josh, but we will be there for them." What was she talking about?

"What? No, Mom he was there, with us, he was there...I saw him...he was running into the woods Mom." I knew I had hit my head, but I know what I saw.

"Okay honey...don't get upset. I...well...I'm not sure what you saw, but if it was Tony, I'll ask him about it...okay? We'll take care of it." My dad said with full confidence. I shook my head still feeling confused.

"I'm so tired, even though I've been asleep for what? Hours?" I said looking back to Tate.

"Reese, I hate to tell you this, but you've been in a coma for three days. You truly were touch and go." The realization of that comment hit me. What if I had died?

"Maybe we should all go and give you a little rest. The doctor said it would take days to get your strength back once you woke up," my mom said standing and patting my hand. Then she leaned in and hugged me. Her tears fell on my gown. "I have thanked God a thousand times for sparing you Reese. I..." Sobs strangled her words. I rubbed her back as best as I could. I loved this woman so much.

"I know Mom. I'm so glad he let me live too. Thank you....I love you." I cried with her.

One by one everyone came up to hug me and tell me goodbye.

"You scared the shit out of me you hussy...now I know you just crave the attention you always get..." Chloe said. "I love you so much...look at what you've done to me...I look thirty with these bags under my eyes." I chuckled..."I'm so glad you are okay Reese. I'm here for you." Good ole' Chloe. At least she's honest.

"I love you too Chloe, foul mouth and all." She hugged me a little too hard and she started crying again.

"Come on Chloe. I'll hold you now...it's fun to see you so weak," Elle chuckled and gave me a sideways glance, and a shrug of her shoulders. "We love you Reese. We'll bring you some goodies now that you're awake," Elle said.

And with that I was alone with Tate.

"Reese...." Tate held my hand and gazed into my eyes. "I thought I might never see those eyes again...those gorgeous, green eyes. I literally died three days ago. I didn't want to live. They said you wouldn't make it." He looked down at the ground then with heavy eyes he searched mine. "I thought of everything I would miss out on, without you in my life.

The wedding we're going to have, the children we'll raise. You know, the little boy with your eyes and golden hair, and my stubbornness." He let out a low cry..."All I could think about is that we didn't get our chance...I prayed to God without ceasing...truly down on my knees Reese." Then he reached up and gently held my face in his hands. "I wouldn't have wanted to live without this," he reached down and gently touched his lips to mine, leaving them softly pressed for what felt like minutes. His tears were melting into mine. "Promise me you would never make me live without you," he said. I shook my head. I couldn't speak. This man loved me to the end of the earth, as I did him. "God is good, he brought you back to me...and us back to this," he bent down and kissed me again.

I was overcome with emotions. I looked at him with tenderness and through teary eyes I said, "Always know that you have the ultimate attainment of me, not Carter, you have...my heart."

We simply stared at each other for several moments... then he sat back in his chair, he didn't take his eyes off of mine and said. "Reese, what Carter said though, he was partly right."

"No Tate, we didn't. I told you I'm waiting for my wedding night. Except for the 'date rape', I have never..."

"That's just it Reese. When he was saying those things to us, I was seeing red. I knew he was lying. But, I had all of this time to think while you were in a coma. Things just didn't make sense. It helps that both of my parents are lawyers, because they were able to pull some strings. Don't be mad, but I had to tell them about what had happened to you...you know the date rape."

"What? Tate no...I...Why?" I was speaking faster than I was thinking, then it sank in that he had to have a good reason..."I'm listening."

"Well, I had the District Attorney pull up your case from back then and look at the DNA and fingerprints. Before they, well...before they prepared Carter's body for burial, they ran his information and...it was a match Reese. He...It was a match..." He dropped his head down low. He looked mixed up, like he couldn't keep up with his emotions.

"I don't understand. What are you saying?" He didn't speak back. Just silence. Then he looked back up to my eyes. I saw tears again in his. This time, guilt and love... Slowly I understood. Flashbacks ran rampant in my brain. Little tidbits of time, all pertaining to Carter. The moment we parted at Elle's party... him in the car waving me over...his words in my ears, when my vision was too blurry. All of it rained down on me. I started sobbing...hysterically. I couldn't believe how I felt. It was a mix of emotions, just like Tate, of sorrow, hate, love, fear, regret, pain, guilt...Carter had raped me and then gone about life like it had never happened. How did I not ever see that? I knew why, I didn't want to think it...ever. Tate hugged me. Without saying a word, I could feel his protection and love caressing my soul.

"Tate, I love you..."

"More than words Reese...I love you more than words." Several minutes later, Tate stood. I think he was mentally and physically as exhausted as me, and I was the one who'd been shot. That reminded me.

"Tate, why does Tony say he wasn't there that night when Carter was shot?" I cringed saying those words. "I mean that was his son, he should have stayed and been with him."

"I'm not sure Reese. But there are so many unanswered questions from that night. As of now, it appears...." Tate swallowed. "It appears you were shot accidentally during our scuffle. And, it appears I caused him to pull the trigger and shoot himself. We were struggling and the gun went off." Tate's inner turmoil showed on his face. "They're calling it self-defense, but the DA still wants to investigate. I may need a team of lawyers by the end, but my parents don't think so. They think it will be okay."

"Oh Tate, I didn't even think that you would be in any kind of trouble. He brought the gun...I saw it." The flashbacks were utterly painful and I got chills just remembering them.

"They...they aren't sure the bullet they found in him matches the one that..." he looked up at me with pain and confusion in his eyes "the one that hit you."

"What? That's crazy..." I said.

Tate stood up again and ran his hands through his hair. "I know. So much doesn't make sense. I, I heard someone else in the woods too. The fact that you said it was Tony, doesn't make sense to me. Why would he be there? Then, with the bullets not matching, it seems someone else might have shot Carter, but they aren't 100% either way. It just doesn't make sense Reese. Unfortunately the DA says one theory is that I have hidden the gun. That's crazy, I wouldn't...I couldn't do that. Anyway..." He looked like he wanted to say something, but instead he started walking towards the door. "I...um...I'm going to get you a coffee"...he managed a slow grin "they have a Starbucks here... Grande, non-fat, 1 pump white mocha latte...with light whip?" he asked. God I loved that man.

"Please." I said with a small smile.

He turned to leave then poked his head back in the door. "Hey, your mom brought your fancy new iPhone, which I'm jealous of by the way, because I want one. Anyway, she thought you might like it to listen to music. I'll be back." And with that he was gone.

I let out a long exhale. Wow, how could all of this have happened? What if they don't believe Tate? I turned on my phone and started to hit the music icon, when I noticed a '1' beside messages. I clicked on it praying it wasn't a message from Carter before he found Tate and me on Lookout Ledge. I couldn't take that, still having a piece of him left behind. It wasn't though, it was John. Dated today...time, 10 minutes ago.

> Reese, thank God you're okay. I heard about everything. That bastard almost killed you. I want to see you, but know, I will wait. Just like I said. Love – J

What the hell does that mean? Then my hospital door opened.

# CHAPTER 25

t was Tony, Carter's dad. "Hello Reese...."

He looked like he had been run over by a mack truck. He had just lost his youngest son, Carter, just days before. He was most certainly in mourning, as I'm sure his wife Lisa, and his oldest son, Josh were. Carter was much too young to die, at 18 years old. But, I couldn't get past him being the one who had raped me and left me. I had never imagined Carter would have done anything so vile in all of my life. I had loved him, after all. I was devastated when he left me, and even more destroyed when I found out he was able to go about life and never let on that he had raped me. He took my innocence...I thought he loved me. What I thought was his love, must have merely been a sick infatuation.

"Tony, what...I mean why are you here?" I said with an obvious look of confusion, and maybe a little discomfort on my face. Why was he here to see me? I've known Lisa for years through my mom, but I've never once spoken directly to Tony. "My parents aren't here right now, but they should be back shortly," I said, thinking that must be why he was here.

"That's nice Reese, but I'm not here to see them, I'm here to see you," he said with a monotone and stern voice.

"Me?" I know my voice was a little to shrill. "Okay, well that's nice of you." What in the world, I was using his same adjectives. He had me a little flustered, I think.

"Yes, I was just checking to see how you were feeling. Lisa has been keeping up with your recovery through your mom, and I just wanted to see for myself," he said. What a strange comment. All of a sudden you're interested in me?

"Well, I had a rough few days it seems, but I'm doing much better now...thank you. And, Tony, I'm truly sorry for your loss, I am." I was...but I was also so torn on why I wasn't as sad now as I should be. I was having a moral war with my emotions. Ever since I found out he was my rapist, I wasn't quite sure how I felt about his death. "Carter and I...I think we were in love once...I can't believe he's gone." I looked down at my hands, twisting my fingers over and over.

"Yes well, I'm sorry you were shot Reese. Your situation could have been much worse. I had no reason to think Carter had a gun...I mean you have no idea how shocked I was by that. Anyhow, Liz says there was some confusion that night, and you thought you saw me there. I just want to say that is absurd Reese. I was at home with Lisa, we both heard of Carter's death at the same time." He bent his head down, silence ensued for a couple of minutes. When he raised his head, his red eyes were filled with tears and mine as well. "I can't believe he's gone... My Carter, he's gone. I never meant...I mean I never imagined I would lose him so young." He said. I was really confused by his comment, but I was overwrought with sorrow for this man. I can't begin to know what it must feel like to lose a child. I hope I never find out.

"There's something else Reese. I....I heard your boyfriend had Carter's DNA looked at for a case that happened over a year ago..." He stared in my eyes, "something you claim was rape back then." Something 'I claim', what does he mean by that, I thought? "Anyhow, I don't know what really happened, I just know Carter was incredibly upset when we left town over his mom and me. I suggest instead of looking for ways to blame the dead, Reese, you see who really is at fault for all of this....I think you'll be really surprised...In my opinion Tate is the reason everything spiraled out of control beginning over a year ago...including your rape, us leaving town, and now Carter's death...I'll never forgive him. Why don't you ask him about it...I was pulling for you and..." he was crying, "you and Carter to be together. He loved you like no other Reese." Then he bowed his head and started crying again. "Tate Justice is no good. Ask him what he did to my marriage." I had heard the whole story of course from Carter and Tate. It just sounded so much more official coming from Tony. "Like I said, Carter was a good son. I don't know what happened...physically...between the two of you. But, I do know he became a different person after Lisa and I split up." He looked down again, his shoulders shaking. The final look he gave me was one of total despair.

I wasn't sure what all he had just said, or what he truly meant by it. But one thing I knew for sure...this man was devastated. Now was not the time for me to argue with him about any of it.

"I'm sorry again, Tony..." I reached out my hand in the air as a token of my sympathy for this man. He merely held out his hand too, then bowed his head and said "Reese, I wish you well," and walked out.

I had never thought of any of this really being Tate's fault. I couldn't think of that now. I just couldn't go down that road. I needed him, and he needed me. I had my hands over my face and was weeping into them when Tate returned with my coffee. He couldn't get across the room fast enough to comfort me.

"Reese, what is it, what's wrong? Did something happen while I was gone?" He had set down my coffee, and sat on the edge of my bed, his hand on mine, and his eyes fixed on me.

"Tony was just here and…"

"What? Why was he here? What did he want?" Tate said, just as confused as I was.

"He says he just wanted to see how I was doing, and tell me he was sorry for Carter accidentally shooting me. God Tate, that still just sounds so weird. I mean, I can actually say I have been shot…" I was still so much in awe of that fact. I had never known anyone to be shot, much less someone my age. "I'm so thankful the bullet hit the upper lobe of my right lung. A few more inches one way or the other…and I might not be here." I choked up on the last words. This was just now actually registering with me.

"Oh God Reese, I'm the thankful one. I can't quit thinking about how you looked that night."

Tate's face turned pale, and he started shaking his head.

"My heart literally stopped beating seeing you unconscious and bleeding on the ground. Your small frame not moving…Your breathing was slow and shallow…I didn't know what to do to save you, so…after I called 911, I prayed." Tate covered his face with his arm. "I was praying out loud as Carter was dying right beside of you. His eyes were open, and I heard him Reese...he started praying...he started praying for...you Reese. I heard him....I heard him." Tate was sobbing, his whole body shaking. I couldn't speak or move. "As soon as I heard that, I knew he was dying...so I immediately told him I was sorry it had to end this way. I was holding your chest where you were shot, and not doing anything for him. So I looked at him and asked him if he was saved and he was barely able to get out that he was....his speech was garbled, but he said he hadn't lived for Jesus like he should, but that he was hoping God would forgive him. Then...then he looked right at me and said he had made a lot of mistakes...but that he had loved you, Reese."

Oh God...I closed my eyes wishing Carter was back alive so I could talk to him again...My counselor had told me early on in my sessions that whomever had done this (my rape), would be 'handled' in due time. I guess she was right. Carter had made a horrible choice and he was certainly handled...The question still was how? How was he actually shot, and by who? Was there a mistake that the bullets didn't match? Maybe they were wrong. Otherwise, there was a missing gun, and obviously a missing shooter. It couldn't be Tate...right? No...Now it was time to protect Tate. I was staring at him...

I couldn't believe what all Tate had witnessed, and what Carter had said and done. My heart was utterly ripped open. I reached out for Tate...this beautiful man who would forever be changed from what he experienced. "I'm sorry you had to see me and Carter like that Tate....I'm so proud of you...for what you said to Carter. I had no idea that in his final moments he would be so...giving. After realizing what he had done to me last year, I wouldn't have thought he was capable of that..."

After a few moments I motioned for Tate, "Please come lay with me Tate. I need you to hold me...please. Life is so fragile. Our life together...we've made a lot of mistakes..." I was crying harder "But I love you...I love you so much." He had climbed in my hospital bed, careful not to dislodge any wires or tubes. As his big strong arms engulfed me, I was covered in his love... There was a peace in knowing we had made it out on the other side of all of our trauma thus far. We would work through our coming problems (and I was sure there would be some...)... But, we would get through them...together.

# CHAPTER 26

Days passed, and I gradually got better. I was finally being discharged from the hospital tomorrow. It couldn't come quick enough. My lung was functioning normally now, and my chest tube was out. I had managed to keep any infection at bay by taking IV antibiotics...luckily. That had been the doctor's biggest concern. My head was still a little bruised, but my headaches weren't nearly as severe. I was ready to sleep in my own bed and be able to sleep through the entire night without interruptions, and strange beeping noises. Tate had just left for the evening. Everyone knew him well, here at Baptist. The nurses adored him. I saw them constantly eyeing him up and down, and trying to strike up a conversation. He had been here every day, hours at a time. I felt SO lucky to have him.

My mom and dad had been by earlier as well. Mom had stayed with me at night in the beginning... before I had officially woken up, and then every night afterwards. This was the first and only night I would stay alone. I was glad she was able to go home and sleep in her own bed. I would be fine, but I had to *make* her leave me here alone.

I was reading a new book, and listening to music when there was a soft knock at the door.

"Hey! So you're getting sprung tomorrow?"

It was Elle, Maura, and Chloe. They were a sight for sore eyes.

"Hey to y'all! Yes, thank God. I will be leaving early in the morning. I can't wait to get back to a normal life. I mean we only have three weeks left before we have to leave for Wake Forest, to move in." I said.

"Don't remind me," said Chloe. "I'm going to be so sad when we are all broken up this fall. Maura is going to hate me by the end of the first semester...I'm sure of it. I mean, she's going to get so sick of me being in her business. After all, I'm so use to helping all of you out..." She and Maura would leave in three weeks for UNC Wilmington...near the beach. I was sort of jealous for that. But, Wake Forest was where Tate, Elle, and Finn would be, and where I would have my scholarship.

"Um...I'm not sure 'help' is the right word for what you do for us Chloe...maybe more like badger and instigate." I said, all of us laughing...except Chloe.

"Hey...trust me, none of you would have been able to survive high school if I hadn't been there to steer you on the 'right' course." She said raising her eyebrows up.

"You mean the wrong course..." She looked hurt, but we were chuckling. "I'm kidding Chloe. We love that you made us take chances...most of the time. But Chloe, you have to promise us you'll think a little bit longer before you act in college. And Maura, don't hesitate calling us if you think she's getting out of control. We'll come and lock her in your room for you." I said. We all hugged. I knew we would see each other several more times in the coming days. But, it just seemed the closer we got to leaving for school, the more sentimental we became.

Chloe got up and started pulling Maura up towards the door. "Hey, come with me...I saw a CUTE male nurse up the hall. I want to go see if I can think of a medical question to stump him with." She looked back at Elle. "Then, we better go guys...I'm sorry, but I need to talk to Brett on the phone before it gets too late."

"Wait...you've been keeping up with him? Is he behaving?" I said. I really wanted to ask 'so how is John then', but I stopped myself. I couldn't think like that.

"Brett's good Reese. He swears he's keeping clean and working all the time. Love ya girl," then she jerked Maura "let's go."

"Bye Reese...I love you...pray for me with this one," Maura said pointing to Chloe.

"I will!...You're going to need it!" I yelled.

"I'll come find you two in a couple of minutes so we can go," yelled Elle. She had driven them here.

"Reese, I hate I haven't had much time to come by and visit. I've been totally wrapped up helping my grandmother... you know, where she had fallen and broken her leg. It's hard on my mom to do it all. So, I was staying with her several days." She came a little closer. "Your color is better, but you still look so thin...We need to hang out at the cabin for a few days and veg out!"

"It won't take long to put the weight back on, I'm sure. I haven't been able to do anything in here but eat. I'll be a pile of mush by the time we leave for college."

"You'll be fine. You could stand to lose a little bit of your perfectness…if it is only temporary."

"Elle, you sound like Chloe!" I laughed. "Listen, I've been meaning to ask you about John," I said.

Elle turned away from me and said "John? What about John?"

I grabbed her hand and turned her to face me "Elle…what have you been doing?" She was looking all around the room, trying to act nonchalant. "I knew it…you've been texting him, haven't you?" I couldn't believe it. But, that explains how he knew.

"Okay, I have…but don't be mad." She cringed and ducked a little. "I couldn't let him worry about you once he found out."

"How did he find out? I mean. He knew within minutes of my waking up. I got a strange text from him," I said.

Elle let out a long sigh. "Oh Reese. I don't know what to say. I can't explain it, but I feel a great need to keep him updated on you. He seems to…require it. He acts like *he* is your boyfriend and like he's just…out of town or something. I don't know. The protectiveness he has over you is reserved for doting husbands…not short term dates. It's strange Reese, but I think he's totally in love with you…or at least the thought of you…He's been texting me daily if not, every other day, to find out how you are. I like him of course, I like Tate too. If Finn was checking my phone, he would be mad at me for texting him so much, even if it was about you. Reese, I wish for your sake and his that he would find someone else…you know…get his mind off of you." She kept on…

"Not long after we got back from the beach he called me to ask a lot of questions about Carter and Tate too for that matter.

I was worried he was going to come see you while Tate was out of town, but he never did."

Chloe stuck her head back in my room, "Elle, come on... we've got to go...I need to get home...bye again Reese. Love ya!"

"We'll finish this later...okay. Love you..." Then she hugged me and took off.

~~~

It was almost 10 pm well after visiting hours and I was still reading my book...but I had already dozed off several times. I must have finally fallen asleep, because the next I knew there was a hand touching mine. I startled and sat up, real quick. Dazed and confused, I looked all over but didn't see anyone. Then I heard a voice behind the head of my bed, where I couldn't see. "Reese, don't be afraid..." But I was, I was terrified...until the shadow left his face...then I realized...

It was John.

Oh my God, John was here. My beautiful beach god...here.

"Am I dreaming?" I said. Somehow, I must have been.

"No Reese," he lightly chuckled "I'm here. I hope you don't mind."

"John...What time is it? How did you get in here?" I was amazed and curious at the same time. His blue eyes seemed even more sparkling than before.

"I talked my way in...I hope you don't mind...I told them I was your brother." Oh my, I blushed...that would be kind of gross...since we have kissed and all, I thought.

"Oh, there's that sweet blush I've been missing." He came up closer to me, and rubbed the back of his fingers down my cheek. "Reese...I couldn't stand it any longer...I had to see you. I was waiting on all of your family and friends to leave.

"Elle, she told you I was alone tonight...didn't she? Otherwise, how would you know?" I didn't know what I was going to do with her...but this time, she had crossed the line.

"She doesn't really have a choice Reese. I basically ask her every question under the sun about you...I know she won't lie...so I eventually find out the truth."

"She doesn't have to answer your call."

"She knows I would call all day, every day if she didn't."

I looked down in his hand. There was a blue box...Tiffany's. Oh my.

"Here, this is for you." He stepped even closer. His familiar cologne was teasing my senses. "I wanted to shower your room with flowers, but I knew you would get too many questions. So, this is a little more subtle." He handed me the box. When I opened it, I felt light-headed.

Subtle, who was he kidding. "I can't accept this John. I... can't." He was opening it up and getting it out. It was three diamond and gold bangle bracelets. If I were to guess, about $20,000 worth of jewelry! "You're crazy...there is no way I can take these...they belong on a movie star, not me...and how would I explain these to Tate? Please tell me they'll let you return these..." I tried to move my arm away, but he grabbed it and slid them on. I dropped my head to my hands and began crying.

"John, why are you still doing this? I...I don't know what to say to you. You said you knew Tate would mess up, but he won't...and you have to know now, that I'm his...and he's mine." John's face turned red, and he looked away, briefly.

Then he reached down and cupped my face in his hands, wiping away my tears.

"I don't mean to come on so strong Reese. This is all I know...money. I see someone different, genuine when I look at you. I see love and maturity...you're an old soul Reese Stanford. I want to get to know you better. That's what I want....what I need. I want to love someone who cares about me...not just for the money, but for ...me. I've never had that before. But I felt that when I was with you. Please take these." I was staring at him...feeling sorry for him. "Consider it a friendship gift, then," he said.

"John, I can't begin to tell you how upset and confused that makes me. I know you think you feel that way about me, but, you can't okay. Please don't. I need you to tell your heart that it needs to move on." I was sad saying the words, because I knew deep down I loved having him feel that way about me. "You know I think so much of you too John, but I could never act on any feelings I have. I respect and love Tate too much..."

John cut me off. "And as far as Tate, he already has screwed up Reese..." John sat by me on my bed, staring in my eyes..."I think he'll be tried for the murder of Carter...I don't see how he can get out of it, even if his parents *are* lawyers." I was feeling sick on my stomach all of a sudden. John kept talking, "I have a lot of attorneys myself and for the corporation. They were able to find out all kinds of information on the charges. Unless the gun and the true killer, if it's not Tate, come forward, he will be charged. Carter's parents were interviewed, and they said he's already fought Carter once. They said Tate hated Carter, and had even said he would kill him before." He had said that, I thought, but only to me...he said he would kill him if he hurt me again. My heart rate had escalated; my eyes were darting around the room. "I'm sorry this is so hard on you." Then he put his arms around me. I was so upset I put my head in the crook of his neck and cried.

"John, please, you have to leave me alone, okay? I...can't see you anymore."

"You don't mean that..."

"**Yes**...she does...get the hell away from her." Tate...I couldn't believe Tate was here, and seeing me lean on John. I wasn't sure what to do.

"I can't believe you're here...how...it's so late...?"

"Obviously, it's not late enough..." He said staring at John. "Didn't she tell you to leave her alone? I expect you to leave now."

John got up, staring at me the whole time, and walked towards the door. "Good luck Tate, you're going to need it." He said, never looking directly at him. Then he was gone... again.

"Reese...what is it with you and him? Do you want him Reese? He's trying to drive a wedge between us...I...I'm not sure I can compete with him." He looked down at the gift box on the bed, then to the bracelets on my arm. "Shit Reese. Did you keep these?" He held up the box, pure pain in his eyes. He acted like he was going to throw it hard, but he didn't release it. Then he carefully set it back. "I'm truly losing it here. I came here to tell you..." He sat on my bed, looking at me with tired eyes... then more quietly he said "I came here to tell you that they're calling me in for questioning in the morning. They have new evidence from Carter's parents that I had threatened Carter before, and they said I probably shot him on purpose, and hid the gun.

My parents are worried sick Reese. I...I'm worried too. Then, I come here and find you in the arms of another man...a multi-millionaire....Ahhh!" He made a loud noise in the air and stood up quickly, running his hands through his hair.

"Tate, come here. Please lay with me. Stay here...with me... tonight." He sat on my bed. His eyes were begging me for confirmation...confirmation that I was still his. I leaned forward and kissed him, lightly at first, then long, and hard. Within seconds, he was kissing me back hard, all of the frustration strengthening his kiss and his embrace.

"Oh Reese, I...need...you...now". He was unraveling right before my eyes. His lips were all over me, kissing my neck, down to my breast, then back up to my lips again. "Please Reese, let me know you are still mine...all of you." His hands were wandering, rubbing my front. I could feel the stress from all of his troubles wound tight in his muscles. I know he needed me...all of me...but I couldn't. Just as I was about to tell him no, the door opened, and in walked my night nurse.

"I'm here to take your vitals, Miss... Oh my goodness. You two can't do that here. Mr., you need to get either in that cot, or leave please. Besides, what happened to your brother Ms. Stanford? He was in here earlier...what a handsome devil he is." Great, make Tate feel worse will you? I thought.

We put our foreheads together to catch our breath. I was sure Tate was reeling from her comment. But he was a gentleman as usual.

"Yes ma'am, we will be smart. I'll sleep on the cot. And her brother...he left already...he won't be back." He looked at me, like he was making me a promise.

As soon as the nurse was gone, he climbed back in bed with me. We were spooning each other. I was comfortable and completely satisfied in his arms...as usual.

"Tate, what are we going to do? Let's forget about John for now." He started to protest. "Please Tate we need to focus on getting you out of trouble. I need you to be okay....I know you don't want to do this....I don't want you to do this, but you need to talk with Lisa...completely off the record. I think there's more to this story. When Tony was here, he was hating on you, telling me you were no good for me." Tate leaned back to look at me with anger in his eyes. I laid back against his chest. "I don't care what he says, I know he's hurting, but some things he said just didn't make sense. I really think he was there the night of the shooting. I saw him! I'm sure of it. You need to find out from Lisa what he's hiding. Maybe your parents could help you with it...you know, record it or something."

I wasn't sure what he needed to do, but he had to be let off. I couldn't stand to think of him being blamed for Carter's death. And prison...I was SO scared on the inside...but I had to be strong for Tate. This was his entire future hanging in the balance and "all for me". I just realized I said that out loud. He turned me to him.

"Reese, this is not your fault. It was an accident...all of it."

I looked at him, "Go Tate...find Lisa...fix this. You can make her tell you what she knows. She's covering for him. Go, now... you know how to reach her. There has to be a way to see her."

"I have to be at the police station by 11 am tomorrow morning. I'll text her and see her first thing in the morning. For now, let's rest. I want to hold you Reese."

I looked up at him. I loved him so much...this time I wanted to protect him. "Tate, let me hold you...please. I need to know you're here with me...all night."

We fell asleep, each of us holding the other. Hoping the nurse didn't come in and beat Tate out of the bed.

# CHAPTER 27

When I woke up, Tate was nowhere to be found. I carefully got up (I was still sore...especially on my right upper chest) trying to see if he had left a note or anything. The door opened and in walked a cheerful Tate, coffee in hand.

"Good morning." He said, handing me my special order coffee, and offering me a soft peck on the lips. "You finally get to go home today. I know you're ready."

"Tate, are you okay? You seem so much better than you did last night. This is a big day for you...I'm worried about you."

"Don't be Reese. I'm going to try to work it out...no, I'm sure it will work out. I texted Lisa how sorry I was about Carter. She's going to meet at the corner coffee shop at 9:30 this morning. So, I'm heading home to talk with my parents first. I love you...wish me luck."

He gave me another swift kiss. Then he said "and I've already spoken to your mom, she's coming at 10:30 am to take you home."

My man, he thinks of everything. "I love you Tate. Please call me when you know something."

"I love you too Reese. Bye." He said walking out the door. I showered quickly and got dressed. I was feeling stronger every day. I was putting my things in my bag, when there was a knock at the door.

"Can I come in?" the voice was a familiar but distant one. Then I registered who it was.

"Josh, come in." Why was Carter's brother here to see me? He looked awful.

"I hope you don't mind me coming by Reese. I...I'm sorry you had to be here...I'm sorry for everything that has happened. I can't believe..." He looked right into my eyes. "I can't believe Carter is gone." He dropped his chin down, clearly trying to suppress his crying.

"Josh, I'm okay now. I'm sorry...sorry about Carter. I can't believe he's gone either. He was much too young. I never knew him to be so violent...you know, to have a gun with him." I said.

"That's why I'm here, Reese. He did have a gun...Dad's gun...and he had learned his violence from...our dad as well." His words were broken and pained. Years of heartache were expressed with each syllable. "I have deliberated over whether or not to come to you, but in the end I had to. It's the right thing to do."

I didn't understand. Come to see me? "I'm glad you came. Were you worried I wouldn't want to see you...what do you mean the right thing to do?"

"I heard Reese. I heard what Carter did to you." He quickly looked away, then when his eyes met mine again, they were red and...and totally sincere. "Carter...he raped you. I didn't know Reese. I'm so sorry. No one should ever have to go through that...I just don't get it. He loved you. I can't believe he would ever hurt you like that."

"How did you know Josh?" I said, unsure how he would have already found out.

"I heard my parents talking about the DNA results and how they matched your records from your case. That's not the only thing I heard, Reese. I heard them talking about the night Carter was shot. My Mom was sobbing, hysterically, so it was hard to understand. They didn't know I was there. But I had just come into town and had used my key on the back door. I had no idea what I would hear when they thought they were alone." Josh paced back and forth. He was over-anxious, and grief stricken.

"Josh, what did you hear?" I was unsure what he was going to say, but for some reason I had an intense fear that resonated deep in my gut. He walked closer to me then. As he did, I could see his hands trembling. He grabbed my arms as if he were really needing me to hold him up.

"My dad...he...he was there when Carter was shot. He... he was yelling at my mom, scaring her into lying for him. He shook her so hard, making her promise to say he was at home with her." Josh was nearly whispering, like he still couldn't believe he was saying these words out loud.

I KNEW I had seen Tony there at Lookout Ledge. I knew it. But why? "Josh, why wouldn't he say so? Why would he deny I saw him? I don't understand." I know my words were running together, but I just couldn't comprehend all of the secrecy.

"Reese...I heard everything. I can't believe he was telling my mother. I guess he really does think she would do anything if he scared her and threatened her enough. Or, maybe he was still in shock himself, and he didn't realize he was even talking." He was shaking his head, still in disbelief himself.

"What...what did you hear Josh?"

"Oh God...I'm not sure about telling you this. I'm not sure about anything anymore. I lost my only brother." Then he looked at me again. His pain was heart-wrenching. "Now I'm about to lose my dad too...I guess the pain won't be quite as horrible as with Carter. My dad has never been a father. He's been our family abuser my whole life, and Carter's too. The only person he ever really tried hard to please was Carter in his sick, twisted way. I think he felt he had a second chance to raise a son better than he had me. In the end...that was the son he killed."

What? "Killed...Josh, what do you mean...emotionally?" My head was spinning. What was he saying?

He paced back and forth again. Then he stopped and dropped on his knees down to the floor. "My Dad murdered Carter...accidentally...he shot him, thinking he was hitting Tate."

I half gasped, half screamed out loud. I threw my hand to my mouth and sat back hard on the bed. My eyes were frozen open, staring at the floor. I slowly raised them to Josh. "Josh, you mean...you mean that's why he was there...he was there to kill Tate?" I felt like I was going to be sick. Tate was almost killed. He was almost gone forever...instead of Carter.

"Yes Reese. He was obsessed with getting rid of him. Ever since he caught my mom and him together, he has despised him. Then, every chance my mom got, she threw it in his face, that she could leave him for someone younger and that she had sex with him." My breathing stilled. He promised me he hadn't slept with her. "Then when Carter couldn't get you back because of him, he figured it was time, time to fix the problem, the problem of Tate Justice. I'm sorry Reese. I know this is hard to hear. I can't believe I'm even telling you. I...I'm so worried for my mom, and so tired of my dad ruining our lives. He KILLED Carter." Josh was sobbing, his head in his hands.

I kneeled down to him and touched his hands. "I'm so proud of you for doing the right thing Josh. I can't imagine how difficult this must be for you." I waited until he lowered his hands. I still couldn't believe what I was hearing. Then I looked him in the eyes. "Are you saying he shot at Tate while Tate and Carter were fighting, and he accidentally shot Carter... in the stomach? Then he ran?"

He was shaking his head yes, "I heard him telling my mom. She was hysterical. She was so distraught. I thought she would die right there in his arms. Her scream was piercing. I wanted to run to her, but I needed to hear what was happening. Thank God I waited. He revealed the whole truth. He told her how you were shot too, and how Tate would be blamed for shooting both you and Carter. I think that news was also devastating for my mom. I know she still has feelings for him. I don't necessarily blame Tate for what happened between them, like Carter and my Dad did. I know my Mom was reeling from the attention he was giving her, trying to help her out. She was so worn down from the abuse, and emotionally living in daily turmoil. Then a young Tate was around to help her start picking up the pieces. God knows, my mom deserves a life better than what she has had. My mom told my Dad several times she and Tate had slept together, but for some reason, I don't believe it. I think she was trying to push him over the edge. He has been so close, so many times."

I felt an instant sense of relief that Tate hopefully had told me the truth. I honestly was more worried about Tate almost being shot that anything else. I kept picturing him lying there bleeding to death...and not Carter. I started crying.

"Reese, I'm sorry. This is the biggest mess...all of it. And if I would've known my sorry ass friend, Skip, had given Carter Rohypnol," his words were a hiss, "I would have stopped him. Please forgive me."

"You didn't know Josh." We both stood up "How could you apologize for what your brother did? I loved him once...Josh. I loved Carter. If he had had a different home life..." I was crying again, "He would still be here, alive, and who knows we might still be a couple. He had a hold over me for so long."

We hugged then, a bond between us forever forged. We had both loved Carter, and we were both hurting. Josh had willingly admitted to the murder of his brother by his own father. Then I quickly jumped back. "I have to call Tate, Josh. He was supposed to meet with your mom this morning to try to find out what was going on with your dad." I knew it wouldn't be as urgent of a matter for him, but I was worried what Tate would have to sacrifice to gain any new information from Lisa. Selfishly, I needed Josh to go to the authorities...and quick. I was also worried for Tate, if Tony lost it again. Would he still try to kill him?

"Will you testify Josh? Will you go to the police and tell them what all you told me?"

"That's why I came here. I know when my *father* finds out, he will hate me forever. I will just have to live with that. He has taken so much from me already. I need to know he can't take my integrity too. Maybe this way, my mom can move on without him....while he's rotting in jail."

I could tell he was still torn by his confession. I would always know Josh was a great man from this day forward. We hugged one last time. I thanked him, and begged him to please talk quickly to the police, before any more time passed. He left then. I immediately called Tate. He didn't answer any of the five times I tried him. So I did the only thing I knew to do. I planned to find him.

I called my mom and said I needed her to come as quick as she could, that I needed to run an errand on the way home. I would have to fill her in quickly about what was happening, and what Josh had said. I would need to get Tate's parents involved immediately, so they could work on getting the charges dropped. It wasn't going to be easy for my mom (and dad for that matter) to hear what Tony had done. They've known the Davis's for years. It would be devastating for them. She'd already learned this past week of how Carter was a match for the DNA. It was a horrible shock to her. For the first couple of days, Lisa wouldn't talk with her about it. She finally said she was sorry, of course, but that 'what could she do, Carter was dead.'

After signing my life away to get discharged from the hospital, I quickly began to fill my mom in. I was a little worried about telling her while she was driving, so I asked her to pull over, when I told her the part about Tony pulling the trigger. She broke down of course. She had similar emotions as I did. Tate could have easily died, and Tony would forever have to live with the fact that he killed his own son. And most of all, Lisa's loss was the greatest...a son, and now a husband. I wanted to say and Tate too, but she wasn't aware of that saga yet. Time would tell how my parents would react to those details. For now she simply thought he was doing it to help Carter out where I was concerned.

# CHAPTER 28

When we got to the coffee shop, I saw Tate's truck and Lisa's Acura. I was apprehensive about barging in on them, but I didn't know what else to do. My mom was still a little confused as to why Tate was meeting with Lisa. I asked her to please stay in the car. I walked in searching each table until my eyes locked on Tate. He was sitting beside of Lisa, with his arm around her. She was crying into his shoulder. His eyes were red, and teary. I wasn't sure what to do. I slowly walked to them, he straightened up immediately.

"Tate, can I speak to you for a moment...please?" I gave Lisa the most sincere look I could, and turned around to wait for Tate.

He quickly came up behind me. "Reese, what are you doing here? Are you okay? I thought you would be heading home."

"I need to see you in private" I said through clenched teeth.

We walked to the side hall, near the bathrooms. I was whispering all that Josh had said to me...then I stepped back and looked at him.

"What...what did Lisa say?" I was worried about what his response would be...he certainly didn't seem shocked.

"She told me everything Reese. I promised my parents would help her with the courts, but that she really should let

Tony take the full responsibility...that she should tell she was too frightened of him to come forward until now. She agreed...but..."

"But what?" I was looking at him with squinted eyes, concerned for how large the 'but' could be.

"But, that she needs me to be there for her. Before she told me everything, I promised her..." he said not looking at me. "I knew if I didn't, and she didn't come through for me, that my life could change drastically anyhow."

What does that mean? How are you supposed to be there for her.? Let Josh help her." I said, not understanding. "I don't think it's a good idea for you to lead her on, Tate."

"Reese, she knows I'm completely in love with you, and that I wouldn't do anything to jeopardize that." I blew out a quick breath, as if to say yeah right. "Please, let's just be happy that she'll testify against Tony," he sighed.

He was right. This was huge, and truly good news for Tate. I would have to find a way to work around Tate being there for Lisa in the coming days. For now, we would move forward. After all, he would be off to Wake Forest with me soon, and she would be here. She needed to let him go already...that was a silly phase for both of them. Age was most definitely a factor, even if she did look half of hers...

⁓

I couldn't believe how fast things happened after that. Thank God. Tate was exonerated for the murder of Carter. Tony was taken into custody on a $500,000 bond. He was at home alone when the police came to arrest him...He had no idea it was coming. Josh and Lisa had gone together to the police station. It was a somber morning...Their world had crashed all around them. Tony was furious with them, calling them liars and traitors. However, when they had the weapon... which Tony had hidden in a drawer in his bedroom, there was no denying it. They also found the TracPhone he had used to text Tate, so the number wouldn't be traceable. He hadn't realized Carter would be there that awful night, he only knew from what Lisa had told him, that Reese and Tate had planned to meet, she thought at 8 pm. Evidently she had come across this information when talking with my mom. I'm still not sure why she told Tony this though.

Tony's plan was to meet him at 7:30 pm and kill him before Reese arrived. The coincidences in the other evolutions of the night were ridiculously that...coincidences. Evidently, Carter had kept a gun on him just to scare Tate, and convince him to tell 'the truth' about him and Lisa in case he ever ran into us together. That fact would never be truly known. My guess is, Lisa had told them that she and Tate had slept together, so Carter believed it. It was probably her way of making it true in her own head.

The trial would be a speedy one. The evidence was clear. Tony would have several charges against him. For one, attempted murder of Tate Justice. I still cringe thinking of how that could have ended so differently. He also would be charged with accidental homicide of his own son. That charge would have a much less punishment attached, since it was totally not planned or executed. All together, according to Tate's parents, Tony would spend at least 15 years behind bars. Lisa could get a divorce granted in the meantime, if she so chose, which I was sure she would. I can't imagine how long it will take for them to put the pieces of their life back together again. I was a little worried about Lisa and Tate, and the time she has asked him to spend with her before he leaves for college. She claims she needs a shoulder other than Josh sometimes.

My mom and dad finally figured out about Tate and Lisa's 'relationship'. It was a disturbing day, listening to them argue. My mom was hurt and disgusted at Lisa. I have a feeling their relationship will never be the same. I kind of hope it won't at this point. I'm just not sure about Lisa...

My parents were upset by Tate's actions, and now a little worried about 'us' as a couple. Although, they understand the power Lisa had over him, and how he would have been tempted. Only time will tell how they really feel about it all, and how it will affect how they treat Tate. My mom shared with me how she worries with Lisa's eventual newfound freedom from marriage, she may pursue Tate as well, making our relationship more challenging anyhow. I would have to agree... reluctantly. Maybe she will find someone her own age to lean on...God let's hope so.

The weekend before we left for Wake Forest, and Chloe and Maura left for UNC Wilmington, my parents had a huge cook-out...a send-off for us. We grilled out steaks, and had corn on the cob, grilled squash and zucchini, potato salad, and homemade peach ice-cream (my mom makes the best). There were so many reasons to celebrate. The last few weeks had been marked with so much tragedy and heartache...it was time to move forward. The world was at our feet, for us to make our mark on it...I was praying it would be a positive mark. Finn was trying to help out by doing his usual, cracking jokes about all the hot women at Wake, while Elle punched him every few minutes. Oh how I loved my friends...

After we ate, and roasted marshmallows in the fire pit, we sat outside by the flames and listened to music. Out of nowhere, there was a thunder clap and everyone screamed. Then just like most summer nights in Penderton, the skies opened, and the buckets were released. We were drenched from head to toe in a matter of seconds. We all took off running for shelter. Most everyone ran to the house...Tate and I ran to the cabin.

We were laughing hysterically by the time we got inside. Our clothes soaked. With everything that had happened, we hadn't had a chance to be close in a long time. But, with Tate's t-shirt stuck to his sculpted chest, and his pants clinging tight to his frame, I was quickly turned on. I reached up and kissed him. Our mouths smashed together, crashing like the storm outside. I loved the feel of his body molding to mine, his warm breath on my face. He stepped back and looked at me...I blushed, realizing my white t-shirt was glued to me, revealing my thin bra and hardened nipples. He gave an approval grin and raised his eyebrows before he threw himself up against me again, his hands sprawled out on my lower back. Our breathing was becoming harder and faster.

All of a sudden the door swung open, and Chloe flung something slimy and gross at us. I screamed and jumped back, looking down to discover a frog was hopping on the floor... trying to escape from the terror of my scream.

"A frog...Chloe!...Really!" I screamed. Tate looked at me and laughing he said, "you want me to get her for you? I'm already wet."

"Sure," I said. "She deserves it." Laughing still, I shook my head. Chloe would forever be Chloe, and I really didn't want her any other way.

I was cackling out loud at Chloe's shrill scream from outside when I felt my phone vibrate. Pulling it out of my back pocket (thankful it wasn't too wet) I saw a new text...John?

> Reese, I'm thinking of you.
>
> I want to wish you luck on your move this weekend.
>
> One day soon I'm coming to visit you. Until then...I'm still waiting...
>
> Love, J

Oh John...


THE END

Catch *Atonement* the next book in the Attainment series due out Fall 2013 on e-books and paperback. Find out if Tate and Reese live happily ever after, or if John finds a way to win over Reese's heart after all.

# ACKNOWLEDGMENTS

I would like to thank God *first* for all of the blessings in my life. I consider this opportunity one of those many blessings.

The writing and creating is fully entertaining to me! So I would **REALLY** like to tell my family how much I appreciate their patience in my indulgence during this process. There were many times I was SO preoccupied with my story, that I was oblivious to…real life. I love that you all support me in this adventure. I also love that you three girls are trying your shot at writing!! It was a joy to see you all sitting around the living room with your computer or pen and paper and imagining your own story. Who knows, maybe one day you will too Jake. The sky is the limit for each of you, Macy, Hannah Brooke, Katie and Jake. I love you so much!

Thank you to my supportive, caring, loving husband. As always our life journey together is sweet and SO fulfilling. Although with our busy lives, at times we don't know if we are coming or going. I love you, and I'm so thankful you're on this amazing, wild ride called LIFE with me!!!

Thank you to my mother-in-law, Patsy and my Aunt Sheila for helping me figure out grammar and spelling all over again. I love that you are avid readers, and knew what to look for in my story-line. So thank you, thank you again!

Thank you to my parents for raising me to be actively interested in EVERYTHING! Thank you also, for raising me to love God and follow His plan. I love you!

Thanks to my brother who has always had this writing thing down pat. Thank you for your loving critique.

Thank you to my friends (you definitely know who you are) for helping me enjoy life and friendship to the fullest.

Julie has spent years in the medical field, the first few years as a Cardiac Specialty Nurse, and over the last decade as a pharmaceutical and medical sales representative. She has gathered mounds of experience both personally and professionally to pour into her new passion…writing. After years of power points in the corporate world, she is trying her hand at romance fiction with her first novel, Attainment, and the soon to be released sequel Atonement. Julie resides in a small town in NC with her husband and four children. She continues working full time in sales, exploring her writing late at night and in the wee hours of the morning when her children are tucked safely in bed.